THE SLAVES OF CTHULHU

THE SLAVES OF CTHULHU

TONY RICHARDS

WEIRD HOUSE

ISBN: 978-1-957121-62-8

Text © 2023 by Tony Richards

Cover Art © 2023, by K. L. Turner

Interior and cover design by Cyrusfiction Productions

Editor and Publisher, Joe Morey

Weird House Press
Central Point, OR 97502
www.weirdhousepress.com

TABLE OF CONTENTS

CHAPTER ONE

SAUQUILL ISLAND

i

Incident Report by Erwin T. McMannis, a Sergeant of the Narragansett Police Reserve, Rhode Island, October 25th 1923:

The station house felt the same way that it almost always did at 11:30 on a Thursday evening, quiet as death and stiller than a graveyard. Our one other on-duty officer was out on horse patrol and I did not envy him the slightest bit, since the brutal chill of winter had arrived early this year -- the worst of it coming this very evening—and a frost was riming all this building's windows. For myself, I was seated at the front desk, checking through a sheaf of warrants which had recently been sent down to us from the larger precinct house in Providence.

Then, without any forewarning, the telephone next to my elbow began to ring. I picked the handset up and placed it to my ear, only to find myself being assaulted by a loud cacophony of frenzied speech, a voice raised in a state of extreme agitation.

After a short while, however, I recognized its accent and its general tone. This was Arthur Beeching, who I had been friendly with for many years and who I'd often visited in his big house off Ocean Road. I knew him to be a generally decent man, except that dire misfortune had descended on him

ﯓ 1 ﯓ

recently. Janet, his beloved wife of almost fifty years, had unexpectedly and quite suddenly passed away, and he'd responded to this tragedy by taking very heavily to drink.

And was this strange outburst simply the horrible result of that, Arthur in the grip of some sort of delirium tremens? I did my best to calm him down, except the man would not be stilled.

"It's gone!" he kept on babbling. "I swear to God, the whole thing's disappeared!"

"What has?" I asked him patiently.

"Sauquill Island!" was his fierce response. "The whole thing's sunk beneath the waves!"

Now, Arthur's house is directly by the shore, affording him breathtaking views of both the bay that leads up north to Providence and the open sea beyond. And naturally, from that vantage point, Sauquill Island can be clearly seen, since it has practically the same dimensions as the far more famous Martha's Vineyard. Except that this was night-time and a wind was picking up outside, and so it might well be the case that the isle was partially obscured. Add to that the fact that Arthur's vision might be blurred by quantities of alcohol, inducing in him also a quite fanciful frame of mind, and there you had the origins of this peculiar and unlikely claim. And I told Arthur so in no uncertain terms and then returned the handset to its cradle.

Except the phone started ringing again a few seconds later.

It was Mary Carver this time, a spinster in her middle forties who also lived directly by the shore, a sane and sober woman who worked part-time at our local library. But to my absolute astonishment, she began telling me the same demented story.

And other phones were ringing now, in the common room and on our secretary's desk.

I only answered two more likewise calls before I was pulling on my peaked cap and my heavy cape, then running to the alley where our wagon was parked and driving frantically and at full tilt toward the coast at Hazard Rock.

ii

From the journal of Jackson Maynard Sampson Sinclair, Boston, Massachusetts, July 5th 1923:

Having stayed to watch the Independence Day parades, I finally took my leave of the fair city where I had lived almost all my life. A taxicab drove me to South Station, where I boarded a waiting train, and I was getting off again at Providence, Rhode Island, just an hour later.

Emerging from the terminus, I hailed yet another cab which took me to the waterfront, where I might catch the ferry to my new-found home. Most of my possessions had already been sent ahead; I only had a small valise with me, and sat down on it as I waited for the boat.

This day was a bright and pleasant one with hardly a cloud in the sky, gulls wheeling overhead and small ships plying back and forth. And the quays—as is usual these days—were alive with industrious activity and populated with bare-chested men from every quarter of the Earth. I took a Cohiba out of my breast pocket, clipped its end and lit it up, and then proceeded to enjoy the spectacle of other people working hard while I was not.

Why had I left Boston, you might ask? I had now reached my thirty-seventh year, had been a part of that city's high society since the age of seventeen. I had attended more parties than a man could ever count, stepped out with more debutantes than I cared to remember, and had drunk such quantities of good champagne—illegally these last few years, since the Prohibition Laws were now in place—that I was quite unable to recall how much. Such is the lifestyle of the only son of America's first family in the diamond trade.

But by thirty-seven and still single, an unfamiliar mood of deep dissatisfaction had begun to take a hold of me. What had I *done*? What had I actually *achieved*? Once that I was put into the ground, what memorial would remain to tell people that I was one time in this world and I had made some kind of difference to it?

I'd never had much interest in the family business. It is a matter largely of pure mathematics, fluctuations in world price and the resulting changes in the margin of profit, and I've never really had a head for that. And I felt the same way about banking and stockbroking, professions that many of my friends were in.

Except that I could write, and recognized that fact. The essays I had churned out at my private boarding school had received fervent praise lavished upon them, and later on I'd even written pieces for the society pages of the *Boston Globe*. And could I turn that skill to fiction now … take my life's experience and work it into some great novel in the same manner as F. Scott Fitzgerald? I had already read both *This Side of Paradise* and *The Beautiful and Damned* and admired them very much. And could I manage something of the same? It had become my fervent hope.

But I was fairly sure I couldn't start on such a task inside my grand apartment up on Beacon Hill. My phone was forever ringing off the hook, my door constantly knocked upon. Some pretty bright young thing was always after me, hoping for a ticket to the gemstone business. What I needed was some true peace and seclusion, and an island seemed the ideal spot.

Martha's Vineyard would have been my first choice—I had stayed there several times—except that this being July, the place would now be thronged with tourists. But I made some enquiries of a fellow that I knew in the realty business, and he suggested Sauquill Island as a practical alternative.

I rented a small house through him and it was ready and waiting for me now. All I needed was the boat to get across.

It finally showed up, a yellow-and-white vessel maybe eight yards long and completely open to the elements, a smiling bearded fellow of around my father's age stationed at the wheel. But the only other crew member, standing at the prow, had such a very curious appearance that I could not take my eyes off him.

The first thing that I noticed was that, even standing upright, he was badly hunched, his back so bent that he seemed like a living question mark. The second fact was that his flesh was of such a peculiar hue that it was quite impossible to guess his origins … not even a color, really, more a patina or a dirtiness, like something filthy had been smeared across his skin.

His forehead bulged, as did his eyes. He could have been no more than five feet tall. He was holding a coil of rope between his misshapen hands, and as the ship drew close up to the dock he leapt across in a flopping motion reminiscent of a jumping frog, landed on the wooden quay and secured the cable round a bollard. That done, he jumped back to the ferry with that same peculiar and scarcely-human motion, then sat down at the sharp point of the prow and curled right up into a ball.

An unfortunate soul, for sure. A fellow who'd been born deformed and quite possibly child-minded too, only able to perform the simplest of tasks and very lucky that the owner of this craft had given him employment.

Climbing on, I finally looked away from him, paid the captain for the fare across, and gave the matter no more thought.

Till later on, that was.

iii

The crossing was calm, the sea glistening softly around us, a few birds following in our wake, although they dropped away halfway through the trip. And before too much longer Marinsberg, the main town on Sauquill Island, was starting to come into view. It seemed no more than a large village really, with houses built of grayish stone and no movement apparent on its streets.

But out beyond its western edge, a curious structure had become apparent. A solid and rectangular block of upright rock, maybe forty feet in height and fifteen feet in width … a huge obelisk or monolith of some kind. And even more bewildering was the aura it put out; the stone looked mostly black and should have absorbed every scrap of sunlight, but instead it seemed to glitter in the still afternoon air and cast off a faint radiance.

"What on earth is that?" I enquired of the captain.

Chewing on the stub of an unlit cheroot, he merely shrugged.

"People here call it The Plinth, and no one knows from where it came. It was standing there before the town was even built, so maybe Injuns put it there."

Except a plinth was merely the base column of a statue, and this thing had no statue at the top. It had to weigh several tons at very least, so how could native tribesmen with their sheer lack of technology move a block like this or make it lift? It was a puzzle which I struggled to work out. Maybe this was one of Nature's jokes on us, a violent storm plucking this whole great rock from off the seabed and then casting it up vertically upon our shores?

The second surprise came when we moved in closer to the dock. Back behind it was a little square with several narrow cobbled streets radiating out from that. And another cab was waiting for us there, but comprising of a two-wheeled buggy drawn by an emaciated and bedraggled-looking horse.

And when I disembarked and walked across, I asked its driver what this antique mode of transport was about. This was the Twenties, for heaven's sake, and brand-new motor cars were everywhere.

"None of them allowed on Sauquill Island, boss," came the amused reply from the narrow fellow in his Derby hat. "Orders of the Council and particularly of Her Majesty."

I had no idea what he meant by that, and asked him to explain as I was settling into the back seat.

"Oh, you'll see for yourself soon enough," was his response.

He jerked the reins and we set off.

We headed up through the winding streets of Marinsberg, our wheels bumping heavily on the cobblestones, and nowhere round me could I see the slightest sign of regular activity. There were storefronts, but their doors were closed, their windows glossily reflective too. And the front door of every house was shut and drapes were pulled across most windows. The place appeared to be quite dead, yet it was well-maintained and neatly groomed. Could it be that its inhabitants abhorred strong sunlight and only came out once the air had cooled, in the same fashion as the Spanish and the Mexicans?

Finally we reached the open countryside and followed a broad dusty lane, lined on either side with trees. I could see wide grassy fields beyond, and stretches of farmland too, a pleasant and bucolic landscape which I took to straight away. This was exactly what I had been hoping for, wonderfully calm surroundings in which I could get some real work done. My optimism rose to a new peak.

Only to be lowered again by a new vision coming up ahead, a huge dark shape looming toward us through the trees. A massive building, as it gradually turned out, surrounded by a tall iron fence, and that with sharp spikes at the top.

I could scarcely believe what I was seeing as the place hove fully into view … had never looked upon a house like this in all my travels throughout the north-east. I had never seen such a place *anywhere* in fact, with one exception to that truth.

A few years back, a friend of mine called Harry Mack had traveled to Japan with his new wife and toured the entire island of Honshu. And Harry had returned from there with simply dozens of photographs taken on his new Box Brownie. They included several of a Shogun's castle, the one-time residence of some ancient warlord. Its upper stories were all thick and heavy wood and had been painted black-and-white. The story at the bottom was of solid stone. The whole grim-looking place had not been built to delight the eye, but rather to intimidate the senses.

And so it was with this place too. Constructed of dark lead-colored stone which seemed to drain the sunlight of its warmth, there was nothing at all handsome about it and certainly nothing delicate. It was harsh and block-like and with curious angles to some of its adjoining walls. Its windows were no more than narrow slits. Its roof looked like a flattened helmet of some kind. This seemed not like a house at all, but rather like a fortress, and the whole place cast deep shadows on the ground which stretched across the whole width of this road.

"And who lives here?" I asked the driver of my cab.

And when he replied I received yet another shock.

"Anastasia Gorsting, boss."

The famous—many might say infamous—poetess and painter, who had disappeared from public view a few years back.

"She had this whole place built from the ground up, boss, when she first moved in."

I kept on staring at the hideous structure as we trundled by it, and to tell the truth I thought my eyes were playing tricks on me. Because the shape of the place—it had a lower wing to either side of the main structure—seemed to keep evolving, the angles of the walls changing position slightly and the windows moving closer to each other, then drifting apart. That could only be a trick of all those shadows and of our perspective. We were almost past the house by now.

"But how," I blurted, "did she get permission to build such a horrid-looking pile in such a charming setting?"

"The Council decides on such things. And she was voted their chairwoman practically as soon as she arrived. The ban on motor cars came into force a few days later."

"She was only a newcomer here, but wielded such great influence?"

"She rules the roost round here, my friend. Which is why many of us call that gal 'Her Majesty.'"

That last piece of information stunned me into silence, and I sunk back in my padded seat without uttering another word. What kind of place had I arrived in here, where a dauber and a disciple of Erato—one with a mysterious past and with a dangerous reputation—took complete control this way?

I had often heard that small communities had strange and even puzzling ways of going about their business, except that this was taking strangeness to the very limit of the word. When I took a glance behind me, the house had become largely hidden by the angle of the trees and was so sunken in shadow I could hardly make its details out.

I decided to put this whole matter out of my head and concentrate instead on the location I was headed to. I was moving into a new home and starting out upon a new phase in my life, and that should be a cause for happiness and excitement, so I did my best to embrace those. We passed several far more normal, typical abodes, and then the house that I had rented came in sight.

On two stories and built entirely out of wood, its walls painted a pale beige, it was a humble but a pleasant structure I immediately took a liking to. Here was the serenity I had been seeking, the gateway to a simpler existence, far removed from the excesses of society, where I could concentrate on prose and finally make something useful of my life.

I climbed down with my valise, paid the cabbie and he trotted off. I had mostly forgotten about the other house by now, so eager was I to take possession of my own.

There was a broad covered porch out front, with two wooden steps which thumped dully as I mounted them. I started fumbling in my pocket for the key the rental man had given me. But then I stopped.

A bicycle, enameled a light green and new-looking like it had just been delivered from the factory, was leaning up against the house's wall beside a little outdoor table and a pair of wicker chairs. And hanging from its handlebars, suspended from a length of string, there was a small card on which a message had been scrawled.

You'll need this for getting around, Mr. Sinclair, it read. *Accept it, please, as a housewarming gift.*

But what really struck me was the way it had been signed, with merely two initials.

A and *G.*

CHAPTER TWO

A DREAM OF THE DEEP

i

Incident Report by Erwin T. McMannis, a Sergeant of the Narragansett Police Reserve, Rhode Island, October 25th 1923:

Something began dawning on me as I drove. An aged and inebriated widower? A spinster of middle years? Why the blazes had they even been awake at close to midnight on a Thursday eve?

Ours is a simple and a quiet community, much given to early rising, days spent at a gentle pace and taking to our bedrooms at a decent time. Indeed—as I pressed on to Ocean Road—all the homes round me were dark, not a lit window anywhere that I could see, their occupants submerged in sleep.

Yet, when I reached the end of Kingstown and then took a sharp right, every single house along the shore was lit up brightly as a Chinese lantern. I could even make out people standing outside in their yards.

So what was it that had woken them? The wagon's engine was vibrating harshly and I could not make out any other sound at first. But gradually there traveled to my ears a constant and tumultuous din, an awful heavy throbbing and a churning noise. It was coming from the ocean past our coast, which was furiously agitated in a way I'd never seen.

Understand—I've lived here all my life. I have seen many mighty storms and whirling cyclones. But even during the worst of them, the ocean behaves the same way. The waves might be enormous but they all move in the same direction, crashing in upon the shoreline with tremendous primal force. Save that that was not the case right now.

It was like some gargantuan hand had stirred the surface of the water up so that it raged hither and forth in all directions, waves colliding with each other, breaking up and then re-forming, the air above them filling up with droplets so that it looked like a pea-soup fog. Never had I seen the sea like this, as though the laws of Nature had been utterly discarded.

My gaze kept hunting for a glimpse of Sauquill Island. I already knew where it should be and normally I would have spotted it quite easily. But the frenzied and unnatural motion of the waves and the resulting haze was making that extremely difficult. I slowed the wagon down and then peered hard, but the isle still refused to come in sight.

There was a dim but quite peculiar color lighting up this entire scene. Directly above where Sauquill ought to be, a mass of clouds had formed into a broad and dizzy swirl, almost like a vortex in the sky. It was rotating swiftly, and was tinged with a hue that should not be there, a sickly, almost luminous bluish-green. As I stared at it I felt a lump form in my throat, since I had no idea what was the cause of this.

Determined to find out what was going on, I sped the wagon up again and pressed onward till I reached Hazard Rock, the best location all along this shore from which to observe the open water. And I scrambled out across its granite ridges till the tumultuous waves were right in front of me.

Of Sauquill Island there was still no sign, but I could make out something else. There among the raging currents, some fifty yards out from the shore, the head and shoulders of a lone man could be seen and he was struggling desperately, trying to swim toward me.

ii

A and *G*. But how'd she even known my name, or understood that I was coming here?

But I had to pause at that point, reminding myself I was no longer in a big city but rather in among a community far far smaller and considerably more intimate. The rental agent would have come and gone quite openly. The delivery men, arriving with my stuff, had doubtless spoken with some locals, and in that way the word had gotten round. So most people around here likely knew precisely what my business was.

I let myself in and switched on a few lights. The house turned out to be only cheaply furnished and looked like it had not been decorated since the end of the Great War, but it had a pleasant smell of old dried wood that reminded me of trips to cabins in my youth. In the middle of the living room floor were two large trunks and several smaller crates, containing all of the belongings that I needed here.

I unpacked my new typewriter first, a Remington Portable No. 1, and set it down reverently on the dining table at the back. My clothes came next; they had been sitting here for several days. I'd had them pressed and wrapped in tissue paper, but still knew that they would crease if they were not transferred to hangers soon. And so I started shifting bundles of them up into the main bedroom, which proved to have a large deep closet.

Warm sunlight was streaming through the window there—by now it was late afternoon. And so I went across and took a good look at the view. The house itself had a small back yard, bounded in merely by low latticed fencing. But out beyond that was an open lea that must have stretched for half a mile, a grouping of tall conifers over to the right of that, and where the green lea finished up there was a swathe of ploughed dirt with a farmhouse set down at one corner of it.

But the whole vista was remarkably flat. That impinged on me with a slight sense of unease. Everywhere that I had ever been throughout the north-east countryside, the ground had always risen and then fell, but the scene out in front of me was just as even as the flagstones out on Harvard Square. Not only no hills in sight but not so much as a small mound. Perhaps strong winds down all the centuries had scoured this section of the island smooth?

Due to a wide bend in the lane that I had traveled down, I could see the backs of other houses from this vantage point, including the rear section of the ominous monstrosity. Not its gardens; they were hidden behind tall dense privet rows. But the back of the structure—just as ugly as the front—had a balcony suspended from its upper level that was surrounded by a parapet of stone. I could not make out anybody on it, but there was an unfamiliar object in plain view ... some kind of large long cylinder, made from brass apparently and angled upward at the heavens. I couldn't figure what it really was, however hard I stared at it, and so I finally turned away and continued with my work.

The light had started fading by the time I'd got my wireless out and set it on the mantelpiece. I switched it on and fiddled with the knob, but everywhere I took the dial I was rewarded with nothing but loud static. Reception seemed to be bad in this place, despite the completely flat surroundings. So I made a bit of extra effort, shipping out my gramophone and a few of my shellac discs, and before much longer the bright rhythms of King Oliver's Creole Jazz Band were reverberating through the downstairs of my brand-new home.

I'd made sure through the agent that the fridge was stocked, but I've never been much of a cook. Two baloney sandwiches with French's mustard sufficed for my evening meal. And afterwards—beneath the kitchen sink—a fifth of bourbon was awaiting me, in an unmarked bottle topped off with a cork.

I poured myself a glass and then remembered—with the air around me still pleasantly warm—that there were wicker chairs out on my porch. And so I wandered casually out of doors, sat down and lit a fresh cigar.

I was facing the sea now and the sun was going down, one of those marvelous kaleidoscope events where the sky on the horizon gets lit up with a variety of pastel hues, lemons, pinks, and even mauves. I enjoyed it quietly for a while, but then I began to notice how utterly silent my surroundings were.

There were no sounds coming from the other nearby houses. Not a murmur, either, from Marinsberg, which was not particularly far away.

But neither could I hear the faintest hum of insects, and that ought to have been present at this time of year. Across the lane from me there was a broad stretch of tall grasses, but no scurrying or buzzing sounds were emerging from it at all.

And no birds wheeled against the heavens, not so much as a solitary gull. As the sun slid away and darkness gripped the land, I found myself being plunged into a world that was as black as pitch and absolutely noiseless too, the light from my open door being the only glow that broke that up.

I must admit I felt a touch uneasy, and I'd never previously been bothered by the dark. But I told myself that I had had a long hard day and that my nerves had to be slightly frayed. I finished up the bourbon, stamped out my cigar and went inside and headed for my bed.

iii

I seemed to be underwater, deeply submerged but still heading down, bubbles drifting past my face. Was I breathing? I could not tell.

Shapes began resolving up ahead of me, all of them tinted heavily with green. One of them looked like a massive globe. And then I made out some enormous flattened blocks, but set together at such bizarre angles they appeared to make no structural sense.

A huge door began opening in one of them, tilting at an oblique angle, sliding away with a hollow rasping sound. And at first, only darkness was revealed.

But then an enormous face came pushing through, the face of some hideous underwater beast and with writhing tentacles protruding from it. And they stretched across and grabbed me by the throat ...

I awoke with a violent start.

My silk pajamas were now drenched in sweat, my face set rigid but the whole rest of me shaking hard. My entire adult life, I'd hardly ever suffered from bad dreams. So what had conjured up this horrible phantasm, and complete with sea creatures too? It must have been the journey on the ferry across, that and the fact that I was on an island now and so surrounded by whole miles of brine.

The luminous hands on my traveling alarm clock told me that it was gone three, so I tried to ease myself back to the realms of sleep. But every time I closed my eyes, those writhing tentacles appeared again. I finally gave up on Somnus and sat up.

Moonlight was streaming through my bedroom window, which had no drapes across it yet. I carefully got out of bed, went across and stared out once again. Everything down there was as still and soundless as it had been a while back, and that fact kept puzzling me enormously. Even back in Boston we had had night birds; but here, in this considerably more rural setting, there appeared to be no similar types of life.

My gaze went to the back of Anastasia Gorsting's home again. Most of it was dark, except that the balcony protruding from the rear was lit up clearly. A pair of French windows gave out onto it, and they were open and rich yellow light was seeping out. There were no shadows on the move that I could see, but the poetess was probably still up.

Lost in recollection of her numerous affairs, perhaps? Or, pen in hand, she might be scribbling down more pages of salacious verse? I am not a very nosy man, but I couldn't help but wonder what she might be up to.

Thoughts like that, though, were abruptly broken up by a very sudden flash, a burst of colored light, and it came not from the house but from the unseen gardens down below. A most peculiar type of radiance, green yet with the strongest hint of blue, leaping up into the night then disappearing almost instantly. But it made me jolt and then blink fiercely. What in heavens had caused that?

I waited for the glow to come again, my whole frame taut, but it did not. Except there was now movement in the sky.

Very distantly and to my right—so far off its general shape could not be ascertained—something was now flapping through the moonlit air. Some kind of bird undoubtedly, and yet it did not seem to move like any normal one. It seemed to undulate rather than flap. Moved more like a scrap of tissue caught up in a strong updraft than a living thing. But I could make out it was heading in this general direction.

And getting lower too, although it stayed as no more than a vague dim silhouette. It finally disappeared behind the patch of conifers and showed itself no more.

Okay, so there *were* night birds on this island after all, albeit that they did not sing. I told myself that that was good and then climbed back beneath my sheets.

Except that my eyes remained open for the longest while, resisting every last effort to make them close. Like something that I could not name had burrowed into my subconscious and was generally unsettling me.

I had no first clue what it was.

CHAPTER THREE

THE ALIEN INSCRIPTIONS

i

I was bleary when I woke up to the clear light of morning but—champagne and partying, remember?—that was not a condition I was unfamiliar with and I bore it with good grace. Breakfast was two hard-boiled eggs and a mug of Java, which I refilled before heading for my Remington.

I rolled a sheet of paper in, lit a Cohiba and clamped it between my teeth, then let my fingers hover just above the keys. I already had a title, *The Belles of Boston*, and a very slim idea of what the first chapter should be. But my hands refused to move.

I must have sat there motionless for almost twenty minutes before I realized what the problem was. Here was I in a brand-new location, yet I had seen very little of it and had no idea of what facilities it offered me. And that lack of knowledge was diverting my mind and leaving it incapable of real artistic thought. So I figured out I ought to familiarize myself with my surroundings first and *then* get down to writing my great book.

This day was slightly hotter than the one before, the landscape steeped in harsh sunlight. I removed my jacket and rolled up my shirtsleeves, and then trundled my new bicycle right off the porch and mounted it. And seconds later I was wheeling swiftly down the lane. I hadn't done this since I'd been a kid and felt elated, old sensations flooding back.

There was no sign of any of my neighbors at the more regular houses I went by. Then the Samurai Fortress was coming into view again and I stared hard as I approached the place. Its windows looked a little smaller than they'd been the day before, and the angles of its walls still looked decidedly odd. But I was past the building in a flash, putting it behind me and continuing on quite eagerly.

The cobbles of Marinsberg slowed me down to a soft jolt. I carefully negotiated the streets of the little town, taking note of every point of usefulness. There was some kind of general store, a butcher and a fishmonger, and what looked like a news dealer with tobacco products in its window too. But there was still no one about.

I found just one tiny church—it looked rather derelict and its wooden doors were padlocked. And there was no slightest sign of anything like a hotel, a restaurant or coffee house. So what did people *do* round here?

I finally reached the waterfront. The sea was calm, but the sunlight reflected from its surface was being fragmented to a blurry haze so that the mainland was reduced to little more than a soft pallid smudge. Gazing at it, I took in the fact I really was adrift and on my own out here.

The jetty I had first arrived on stretched out emptily ahead of me, but there were further rows of boards to either side of it, and tethered to them were some rowing boats that bobbed on the low waves like children's toys. Apart from that, my surroundings were bare. There were no stores around the square behind me, no chandler's and no one selling bait or tackle, not at all like any other coastal place that I had ever visited.

Except there was a sudden noise back there. In a row of small cottages, some thirty yards off from the quay, a front door had come open and a face had begun poking out. It was that of an extremely old woman, her sparse gray hair tied back into a bun, her shoulders deeply hunched, her almost colorless face so wrinkled it was like a shriveled mask. She was staring down at first, but then she looked up and she noticed me. And I saw her eyes widen, and she slammed her door shut.

So the people here … were they afraid of strangers? In which case, I'd have a hard time making friends. She had been awfully decrepit, though, and advanced age of that kind can play curious tricks inside a person's head, and so I didn't let it bother me too much.

I stood my bike against a nearby post and walked out on the creaking jetty. And when I glanced off to my left, that weird monolith came into view again, still throwing out a strange glitter against the morning air.

And the sight of it plain fascinated me, and so I headed for my bicycle again.

ii

Before much longer, I was not on any proper road but rather on a stretch of rutted tracks that made my large wheels quiver and shake. Tall dry grasses—like the ones out front of my own house—now surrounded me, punctuated by the odd low bush. Nothing in the tiniest bit went scuttling out of my way, and a curious realization gradually occurred to me … that I'd not even heard a dog's bark since arriving here. Save for the taxi driver's sorry-looking horse, Sauquill seemed to be devoid of animals or wildlife, however insignificant or small.

The Plinth was further off than I had first supposed, its size distorting my impression of it. I peered around me as I rode and—as with the view from my bedroom window—the landscape surrounding me was still utterly flat. I could not see how that was right; an island, after all, is nothing but the peak of a submerged mountain, the main part hidden underneath the waves, and mountain peaks have features, surely? So what had caused this quite unnatural evenness? Perhaps some glacier from the Ice Age had simply sheared its contours off.

I finally reached the monolith. It cast a shadow on the ground so heavily that it seemed to my gaze like a rectangular hole, bottomless and ominous and so much so I took some pains avoiding it. I set the kick-stand on my bike and then approached the great stone block.

The mineral was of a type that I had never seen before, almost black but with a greenish tint and with a soapy quality to its smooth surface. But as I drew in closer, I could see that it had golden flecks in it which captured the light and shone. *This* was the source of the radiance I'd seen.

A kind of jade perhaps, or maybe onyx? I was not entirely sure. But something else became apparent. Not all across it but at certain points, hieroglyphs had been engraved into its face.

Very weird ones, quite unnatural-looking. I was far from being an expert in such matters, but I'd visited a couple of museums in my time and I was fairly certain that these hieroglyphs were nothing like the type I'd seen on native artifacts and totem poles. There were no sharp edges and no angular cross-sections in the manner of an X or W. Only swirling, curving strokes, all wandering back and forth with a sinuous fluidity. Which should have been attractive in itself, except I felt a faint repulsion as I gazed upon these shapes. They looked completely alien, like no human hand had ever etched them into that dark stone. As though they'd been created in the lowest depths of the surrounding sea.

But ... shadows bothering me, and etchings too? I stopped, breathed hard and got a firm grip on myself. We Sinclairs were made of sterner stuff, so I stepped closer and pressed one palm forward.

The Plinth felt slightly warm and it was mildly greasy to the touch. But there was something else as well. I believed I could detect a very soft vibration running through it, and could think of nothing to account for that. I paused a moment to be sure, then lifted my hand away.

I had come here out of curiosity, but it had been in no way satisfied. The Plinth, in truth, seemed more mysterious than ever, rearing boldly over me with one of its upper corners partly blocking out the sun.

When I stepped back, I noticed I'd been standing not on grasses anymore but on a mineral formation of a different kind. The rock floor which surrounded the whole Plinth was a pale gray and heavily stippled, and it seemed to thump dully under my feet. I stamped on it and heard it echo with a kind of hollow resonance. So was there some sort of cave down there? But I could see no opening.

Out on the broad ocean beyond here, the yellow-and-white ferry was coming in again. I watched from a distance as it docked and then dispatched its small cluster of passengers—a family; a man in a fedora hat, a rather portly woman and their three young kids. They did not look as though they lived here but were simply visiting. But there were no hotels around these parts and not even a small café, so I did not imagine their excursion would last very long.

I dragged my attention back away from them. I'd set out this morning to explore my new surroundings and I'd partially done that, except that one big mystery still remained—my neighbor in that hideous manse. How could I find out more about that woman?

I glanced across at my new bicycle again and I saw the answer there. She'd left it for me as a gift. And politeness demanded, surely, that I thank her.

I was finally going to meet—with any luck—the fabulously wealthy and notorious poetess who people round here called 'Her Majesty.'

CHAPTER FOUR

THE INFAMOUS POETESS

i

Back on the lane and getting closer to the house, I ran everything I knew about Miss Anastasia Gorsting through my head.

She had to be now in her middle years, had never married and so had no child. Her paintings and her books of poetry both sold extremely well, but they could not nearly account for the great riches she possessed. Rumor had it that her real name was not Gorsting, that she was in fact descended from a branch of Russian royalty who'd, almost presciently, decamped to this country many years before the Bolsheviks had come.

I'd never seen one of her actual paintings, but had heard they were a bizarre form of Cubism, one that did not fragment time but rather meddled with the viewer's sight, depicting surfaces and planes at such unnatural angles that they induced a light-headedness in most people who looked at them. Why anybody would buy such a thing and hang it on their wall was quite a mystery to me, but people in these modern days were always up for something new.

As for her poems—the chief source of her fame—they were always epic, many pages long, and so I'd glanced at a few paragraphs but had not read an entire one. In a similar style to Christina Rossetti, they were drenched in obscure mysticism, redolent of dark fable and of distorted dreams, soaked with doomed Romanticism, sybaritic, carnal too. Tragic sweethearts took each other's lives, hoping for a better life in the hereafter. Proper married women coupled with wild satyrs. Lovers would come back from beyond the grave, and beautiful archangels were watching all this horrid carnage.

Noxious bilious garbage then, except it had a massive audience. Entire large crowds would constantly turn up whenever she appeared for a reading or a signing. A few silly schoolgirls, inspired by her scrawl, had even attempted suicide, screaming out loud that all they wanted to do was to worship her. And several of the Southern states had banned her books and had them burned. As any wised-up person knows, that only creates extra interest and her sales were absolutely huge.

But it was not only her work, it was her way of living too. Every time that she went out to some grand ball or some society event, it was with a different partner on her arm, and sometimes not even a man. And—though it never got reported in the press—word would circulate about the 'parties' that she threw inside her mansions in Manhattan and in San Francisco. The cocaine spilled like snow, apparently, and there were other drugs as well, and people's morals slipped away entirely, along with their clothes.

And yet it had all stopped three years ago. Miss Gorsting had vanished from the public's view. And no one knew where she had gone. But now I did. I kept on pedaling.

ii

The dark bulk of her house came up, and the tall iron fence surrounding it. But there was a gate in the latter, and to my surprise it was hanging slightly open.

I left the bike behind again, my shoes crunching on multi-colored gravel. Three broad steps took me up to the front door. And a bell-pull was hanging to one side, so I reached out and yanked on it.

I had actually become a little nervous, wondering what I'd be confronted with. Her photographs depicted her as quite attractive only not in a conventional way, decidedly tall and with a slightly mannish face, the features firm with a proud chin, long black hair framing all that. 'The up-to-no-good Witch of the East,' one wag I knew had dubbed her. But she was older now and most probably lived a quieter life. And in what ways might that have changed her? I had no idea.

The door came swinging open, and I straight away found myself presented with a most bewildering sight. The man standing before me now was dressed up in a butler's uniform but—standing at five seven at the very most—he was so stocky that the black sleeves of his jacket bulged and the shoulders strained, as did the buttons on his chest.

His face was brown with the faintest hint of yellow. His nose was flat, his cheeks were broad. His hair was black and straight and cut to a stiff fringe. This did not seem to be an Oriental I was looking at, nor a native from around our shores, but rather an inhabitant from further south, a descendant of the Maya or Aztecs perhaps.

His irises were black as well. They battened on my face, then moved over to the bicycle I'd left beside the gate, and he nodded with swift comprehension.

"Mr. Sinclair." His voice was deep and clear. "But, sir, what brings you here?"

"Is the lady of the house at home?"

"Don't call her that, she doesn't like it. 'Lady' is too weak a word."

"The woman of the house, then? Or the mistress?"

"That will do."

And—without uttering another word—he turned away from me and started in. It seemed that I was expected to follow, which I did with something of a furtive urgency.

But the very moment I had stepped inside, a curious sensation came over me. Something like a bout of vertigo, leaving me off-balance like the axis of the world had shifted. And when I blinked, a set of tentacles came writhing up in the darkness behind my lids.

It only lasted for a mere couple of seconds before my equilibrium returned. But what had caused it in the first place, panic? That was not like me at all.

I could now see that the interior of this house was more luxurious than you could ever guess from looking at its outside walls. This was a broad lobby I was in, and there was furniture in the style of Louis Quinze, a huge crystal chandelier depending from the ceiling, ormolu-framed mirrors and a good number of paintings too, though none of them seemed to be hers. I thought I saw a Degas ballerina, and a sketch by Monet too. I might not visit galleries that often, but I've looked at such artwork in books.

The butler was going up a broad and winding staircase and so I continued after him, my pace speeding up a touch. Open doors went past on the next floor, revealing sumptuous bedchambers within. But we were still heading up.

We finally wound up at the opening to a room completely unlike the rest, long and broad and with a parquet floor and with bookshelves all along the walls. There were several small desks. There was an easel too, only with no canvas on it. And the three paintings on show in here were very likely by the owner of this place and indeed—when I glanced at them—my sense of imbalance came back. I looked away and stared ahead.

The French windows were open at the room's far end. And—with her back to me—the mistress of the house was outside on the balcony, both hands planted on its parapet. She had on a deep blue long-sleeved velvet dress that reached down almost to her ankles. High-heeled shoes were on her feet ... indoors, and not expecting company? And she was just as tall as she had seemed. I couldn't help but notice there was a small streak of whiteness in her lengthy ebon hair.

Beside her was the same cylindrical object I had seen from my back window. And it turned out to be a good-sized telescope, mounted on a tripod and tipped toward the skies. So did she have an interest in astronomy? I'd not known that.

She seemed to sense that we were there. Her head tilted but did not turn.

"Thank you, Cuesto. You can go."

She was obviously speaking to the butler, who nodded and departed, heading quietly down again. I crossed my hands in front of me, my fingers knotting rather tightly.

"Mr. Sinclair? Why the visit, on your first day here?"

Her voice indeed had that slightly purring tone you associate with Slavic speech, though only a faint trace of it. But how'd she realized who I was without so much as even looking round? I guessed that visits of this kind were rare, so she had figured this thing out. A clever woman, then, who relied on her instincts.

"I simply thought that I'd drop by and thank you for –"

"But you can buy a thousand bikes and throw them in the ocean the same day. No, Mr. Sinclair, you did not come for that. You came to take a good look at the infamous mad poetess who used to go to bed with whoever she liked. But you're too late and those days are behind me. I devote myself to finer causes now."

And with those words she finally turned around, and I received a severe shock. Her face was broadly the same way as it had been depicted in the press, but her left eye was covered with a patch, black and with some silvery kind of needlework. And there was a scar down her right cheek, and I had never noticed such inflictions in her photographs. So what had befallen her while she'd been here? I felt awkward, uncertain where to look.

She seemed to understand that and smirked broadly.

"Not the vision that you were expecting, no? But time moves on and it spares none of us." She gestured to me with a swift flick of her chin. "Why are you still standing there? Come join me, please."

I tried to relax myself and started walking forward. And as I got closer to her, well, I noticed something else. Her left hand was down across her hip. But the smallest finger was missing, just a stump remaining there. And how had she managed to become inflicted with yet another injury as severe as that? It was, all told, a worrying puzzle.

I stepped into the open air. This balcony was like the prow of some great ship, jutting out toward the open countryside. There was a glass-topped table to the left of me on which were placed a glass of dark red wine, an open pack of Gitanes, an ashtray and a silver lighter. And the woman lit a smoke and offered one to me, and shrugged when I declined. She lifted the glass of wine and downed it in one go.

"That doesn't look like hooch," I pointed out.

"Chateau Cartier, smuggled in directly from Bordeaux. I get what I want and when I want it."

Right up close, she seemed to tower over me—I had to remind myself that she was wearing heels. The silver needlework on her eye-patch was clearly apparent now. It was a symbol not unlike those inscriptions I had seen on the Plinth, and I wondered why she'd chosen that. But her one good eye, it was the most luxuriant shade of green, a rich and almost shining emerald hue that seemed to have tremendous depth to it.

"Prohibition. Such a silly law," she was now saying, almost to herself, "But then most laws are. Do you not agree?"

I wasn't sure I did, except before I could demur she changed the subject altogether.

"You've been having a good look around? And what do you think of our island?"

"It's quiet."

"Yes."

"And very flat. And ..." I ventured carefully, "there doesn't seem to be much living here apart from people. Almost nil, in fact."

"We're cut off from the continent, and by strong currents too. And there are places in this world that even birds avoid. The flatness of the landscape leaves them vulnerable, but maybe there is something else? Even some rocks have a vital charge, and maybe wild things shy away from it."

Which didn't sound right to me, but I wasn't much inclined to debate it with her. So I leaned across the parapet and stared down at her grounds.

They were the size of a couple of polo fields, bounded in by those tall privet hedges, and were generally conventional in design, some flower beds here, a row of dense rose bushes there, some ivy and an arbor and a white-painted gazebo too, all linked together by a series of pink slate paths.

But at the very center there was nothing but a broad green lawn. And one section of the mown grass—some fifty feet wide and circular—seemed to be a little elevated, bulging slightly higher than the landscape all around.

"So *here's* a part of Sauquill that is not completely flat."

"There's an exception," came the quick reply, "to almost every rule."

iii

I realize now that it was not merely a slight bulge I was looking at. That it was not covered with grass, and it had massive cryptic symbols etched on it and was mechanical in nature too.

But I was already falling underneath the influence of that dark priest who inhabits the ocean's depths. And—slumbering in his ancient home—he reaches out with his inhuman mind and probes into our thoughts and dreams, touching us not physically but by means of his mighty mental force.

Mostly we are unaware of him. We put a sudden burst of violent thought down to our own primeval nature, and an abrupt descent into profound gloom we attribute to the circumstances we are in. But that is not always the case. It is the alien telepathy of Lord Cthulhu brushing up against ourselves.

Except that on this particular occasion, his dire influence was greatly more. He did not *want* me to see the actual dome. Did not *want* me wondering what might be hidden underneath. And so he reached directly into my far weaker brain and made me see just greenery and a slight bulge.

The Great Old Ones ... they have their secrets and they hide them very well. Perhaps it is better that we do not know.

iv

I started asking Anastasia questions, and she answered them without the slightest pause.

Why had she left those two major cities and come here instead?

"I grew tired of other people's expectations, and I came to understand I was no longer living for myself."

How had she managed, and so quickly, to head up the local council?

"People know a natural leader when they see one."

What had she been doing in the way of art and poetry since she'd moved here?

"Experimenting, trying out new ways of doing things. I've even thought of attempting to create a new language."

Okay. And what was it with the telescope?

Her one good eye gleamed pleasantly.

"The skies round here are often very clear. And, looking up from this exact same spot, I saw that they contained a form of artwork human endeavor cannot ever match. The constellations and the individual stars are all more beautiful than we could ever dream about. We are their children, and we cannot be the only ones."

"You think that there are other lives up there?"

"There *has* to be. And older, wiser, and far mightier than us. We are but mere newcomers in this ageless Universe."

All the while that we were talking, I was aching to ask her what had happened to her face. I knew nothing about her left hand, since it had not appeared in any photograph. But I'd seen pictures of her face aplenty—there had been no eye-patch and no scar. Except that kind of question never left my lips, because I'd been brought up to observe one simple rule: when you think to make a comment on a woman's appearance, it ought to be favorably or not at all.

Anastasia asked me not a single thing about myself, and when I tried to turn the conversation round that way she swiftly adopted a bored, dismissive air, lighting another Gitane, turning her back to me and peering off into the countryside. I'd almost been half-hoping that we might be friends, but it didn't look like that was going to happen.

"I'm getting rather tired now," she said quite sharply.

"Okay. Sorry. One more thing?"

"Yes?"

"Why the ban on motor cars?"

She blew smoke out across the hot still air.

"They remind me of the times we're in, even the racket of them passing by. And I yearn for an earlier and simpler age, when we were more in touch with our true natures. You can show yourself out, Mr. Sinclair."

And, still gazing away from me, her frame became as motionless as some marble frieze might be. I had been dismissed and that was that. I stepped away uncomfortably, finally turned on my heel and headed through the room again.

Of the butler, Cuesto, there was no longer any sign. But someone else was at work on the landing of the second floor—a formally attired maid with a feather duster in her hand. A Chinese woman somewhere in her forties, short and squat, her face a mass of ridges and uneven lumps and set into what seemed to be a permanent unhappy scowl. She glowered at me a moment but then—like her mistress—contrived to pretend that I was not there.

Reaching the foot of the stairs, I halted and looked up again, a sudden instinct taking hold of me. High above me, almost back where I had been, a face had appeared between the railings and was staring down.

A woman's face again, but not the owner of this house. Her hair was just as black but it was loose and tousled. Her features were a pale oval. It was too far away to be entirely sure, but she seemed young and quite possibly pretty. I thought I saw her blink at me, and then she turned away so quickly that I caught a glimpse of swirling white chiffon.

Not another servant, then. But who … a friend of the poetess, or even a lover, maybe?

There were too many mysteries about this place, only that knowing of Miss Gorsting's reputation I should have expected nothing less.

I went back out across the front courtyard, remounted my bike and made it quickly to my home.

CHAPTER FIVE

THE MISSING ONES

i

At least I now had a fresh character for my novel. Anabella Goulding (I might have to change that name later on to avoid lawsuits), a middle-aged society doyenne, arrogant and self-obsessed, who treated everyone around her like some deck of cards that she was shuffling to her own advantage.

I tapped away at the keys fairly happily for perhaps the first ten minutes, but then started realizing how difficult this fiction-writing business was. It was made-up but had to seem completely real. Every paragraph I wrote had to be valid in itself yet still had to relate to every other paragraph. I could not keep repeating the same phrase or word, and when my characters spoke they had to sound quite natural but interesting all the same.

I stopped, folded my arms in front of my chest for a while, then ripped the sheet of paper from the roller, screwed it up and threw it on the floor and tried again.

And I was still there by the time the angle of the sunlight through my windows had begun to change. I had managed two and a half pages but could see they needed much revision. My head was blurry and my back was tight.

Holy God, no wonder F. Scott Fitzgerald had some problems in his life. I stood up, tried to unstiffen my limbs, then went and poured myself a bourbon.

Supper this evening was pickles and a sliced-up tin of Spam. But I was starting to discover something else about this writing game. Even when you were no longer sitting down, even when your fingertips had stopped their pounding at the keys, your mind kept working on the story and would not let up, and the fact it kept on doing that exhausted me. So I put on some more records and I played them long and loud.

All tunes have to come to an end, though. The final bright chords died away, to be replaced by just the hissing of the stylus on the disc. It was now totally dark outside, and when I switched the gramophone off the absolute silence I'd experienced last night came oozing in, as dense and as featureless as tar. It seemed horribly unnatural for any place to be as quiet as this. I'd finished almost a full quarter of the bourbon by this stage.

And in that partially inebriated state, I went wandering up the stairs again, stripped down to my underwear and rolled into my bed.

I did not dream of squid-faces or tentacles this time. All that I remember is my dreams were very featureless ones, as dark as the night outside, and the only thing that I could make out was a single eye staring at me.

A rich and almost shining emerald green eye that appeared to have tremendous depth to it.

ii

Because of that unnerving dream, I woke up the next morning with the strong persistent feeling I was being watched. I rubbed a hand across my face and tried my best to banish that idea from my mind. Dreams and reality ought not be mixed, since madness lies in that direction, and I told myself that several times.

The next few days were uneventful ones. I worked on my novel—it was getting slightly easier now I'd taught myself the basic rules. I did my best to feed myself. I went for long rides in the open countryside, not once encountering any type of slope. I listened to jazz and I slept.

But there is such a thing as entropy. Supplies deplete and then run out. And that was the case with both the food inside my fridge and with the bourbon underneath my sink.

That second problem was resolved quite unexpectedly when—going out onto my porch one bright-lit morning later on—I noticed two objects beneath one of the wicker chairs that had not been there previously. They turned out to be a pair of bottles of Irish whisky with the Bushmills label still on them, and one of those labels had a short message scribbled on it. *Slainte. AG.*

My first dilemma, though, could only be resolved by going to the stores in Marinsberg, and I saw that as my chance to meet the people of this quiet flat place.

A small bell tinkled just above my head as I stepped in through the entrance to the general store. A man and woman were both stood behind the counter, and they could have been a brother and a sister, so similar was their appearance. Both were short, with pallid skin. Both had heavy shadows underneath their eyes. They appeared to be round forty years of age but had a sluggish weariness to their demeanor that made them seem a whole lot older.

They did not smile or even look at me too much, leaving me to find the items that I needed by myself. Their gazes wandered off into the empty air instead, like they were seeing things that I could not. In fact, their whole manner was like they'd barely woken up. Slightly angrily, I finished up, dumped my heavy basket on the counter, paid for my provisions and went off, with barely a single word passing between us.

And I got a similar lack of reaction in the butcher's shop. The man behind the marble slab was broad and stout, and yet he had a flaccidness to everything he did, as though his vital juices had been sucked right out of him. Once again, he barely spoke. And he kept on staring at the ground, and there were shadows underneath his eyes as well.

Thank heavens for Mr. Arnold Sewell, the proprietor of the news store, who greeted me with a cheery "Morning, sir" when I walked in.

A thin man in a striped shirt and with a straw boater on his head, he smiled then, with a broad gesture, invited me to take a look around his place. There were numerous books and entire racks of magazines and tobacco products along the back wall.

But no newspapers, not a *Boston Globe* or *International Times*. I pointed that out and he pursed his lips apologetically.

"Not much call for them round these parts, sir." He was rather pale as well, despite his manner and his cheerfulness. "The people of this island, they prefer to concentrate on their own lives."

Which were apparently lived out in a part-hypnotic daze, though I decided to be tactful and I did not say that.

Wandering round, I chose a copy of *The Tatler*, found a simple book on cookery, then asked him for a half a dozen of his best Cuban cigars.

"You'd be the new feller, wouldn't you, who's moved in near Miss Gorsting's house?"

"That's right. I've even met Her Maj."

"Then you know more than I do, sir. She's never once been inside here." Then he took on a thoughtful look and dropped his voice to a much lower pitch. "But would you like anything else? I've got some different kinds of magazines around the back."

And what did he mean, girlie stuff? There was a knowing twinkle in his eye. Except I've never gone in too much for that kind of entertainment … why just look when you can touch? I shook my head briskly, but I thanked him before I left.

Idly, my purchases swinging from a bag around my handlebars, I cycled back down to the quay again. Open water draws us in like nothing else upon this Earth—we feel impelled to stand by it and stare at it, perhaps remembering our prehistoric origins. And the ferry had pulled up to the dock again, and a few more passengers were climbing off.

Among them was a young couple in the late years of their teens who were both well-dressed and remarkably handsome, the boy blond and in a three-piece suit, the girl red-headed in a long pink dress and with a matching parasol. He helped her courteously off the deck, put an arm around her waist, and they went wandering off into the town. Two day-trippers certainly, only here for a brief visit, their hips pressed together as they moved and obviously very much in love.

I watched as they were swallowed by the cobbled streets, then swung round and pedaled home. And did not give the matter any further thought till two days later.

iii

Trying to write my book was placing such a strain on me that I had finished up all six cigars within that period. I pushed down to Sewell's place again and replenished my supplies, then noticed that the ferry had come in once more.

Climbing off it this day there was not the usual type of passenger but three men in the uniforms of the police, wide peaked caps on their heads and bright badges on their chests. And the one who appeared to be leading them, a hefty fellow with ruddy cheeks and with a strong wide chin, had three chevrons on his sleeve. But what could have brought them here? I watched numbly as they approached.

"You live round here?"

"I have for a short while, yes."

"I'm Erwin McMannis," the sergeant said, "of the Narragansett Police Reserve."

And he reached into his pocket and produced a slightly crumpled photograph.

"Have you ever seen these two?"

Despite the fact it was a monochrome shot, I recognized the couple in it straight away. These were the pretty, enamored boy and girl who had gotten off the ferry two days back, and I immediately told the sergeant that.

"They're Michael Seward-Simms and his fiancée, Helen James," he informed me, "both from decent families and scheduled to be married soon. So far as we can tell, they traveled all the way out here, but they have not returned as yet."

Only there was no place to stay here and I told him that as well, and also introduced myself. The man looked weary and bemused, pushing the peak of his cap back.

"There's nothing else for it, then. We're going to have to split up and conduct a search."

With just three men and not even a dog between them? I offered to help and that was gratefully received.

"There's a beach off to the west of here—I saw it from the boat. Maybe they've been sleeping on it, or got lost. Could you take a look, Mr. Sinclair, while I and my colleagues search elsewhere?"

Before too much longer, I was cycling down the rutted tracks again. An abrupt summer breeze had started up, plucking at the tall grasses around me. Over to my left was the high bulk of the Plinth, still casting out a glitter in the fierce sunlight, although it seemed to me as though its elevation had been shifted and the thing was leaning at a slight angle by now. That could not possibly be right; it was so huge and heavy it could not be moved. But, just like the dark house and those unsettling paintings, it was playing tricks on my perceptions and I contrived to ignore the wretched thing.

I finally reached the beach. The breeze was stronger here, forcing the taste of salt into my mouth and churning the incoming waves into a white-tipped froth. The sand out ahead of me was pale and flat and looked, at first, like it had never once been walked upon. What was it with the people of this place, that they didn't even come to take a stroll in such a pleasant spot as this?

But then I caught sight of something, over to my left again, that might well be some kind of narrow trail. And when I reached it, sure enough, there was a double row of naked footprints, two sets of them side by side, emerging from the bank of tall sea-grasses at the beach's rear. Young Michael and his lady-love must have walked through this way and then slipped their shoes off before stepping out.

But where exactly had they gone? They'd seemed so happy that one time I'd seen them, so adoring of each other, and perhaps that sight had burned an image in my brain, since I felt deeply concerned for them.

Their prints led in the direction of the tideline, then turned left and headed down to the shore. Except this stretch of the coastline was curved and I could not make out the whole of it from here. I followed the tracks carefully, glancing round me once in every while. Far out on the sea, a dark head popped up briefly from the waves, then disappeared again. So what was that, some kind of seal?

I went around the beach's bend. The sea-grasses were rattling fiercely now and the waves were coming in with slightly greater force. The footmarks in the sand continued normally for some two dozen yards or so … but then they started to become haphazard.

Something—what?—had driven the young couple violently apart. His slightly larger tracks now veered inland, only hers were heading back the way they'd come, her footfalls wider than they'd previously been, like she had started running. And other sets of prints were descending on them both—half a dozen of them from the grasses, some of them bare and others shod. But even more peculiar, there were three or four emerging from the waterline as well, and they were large misshapen ones.

The sand at one point had been heavily disturbed, flurried about as though by savage struggling, and I found myself looking at drag marks too, like somebody was being hauled along and leaving those impressions with their heels.

The young couple had obviously been ambushed, though by who or why I could not tell. But fear and panic started overcoming me. If they could be attacked, why not myself? Was this place even safe ... was I in danger here?

I froze at first, peering around wildly at the waving grasses and the lashing sea. But finally I registered the fact that I was still alone and started moving quickly, running back toward my bike, then riding furiously to the town again.

iv

I'd expected McMannis and his people to be still split up and searching through the winding streets. Instead of which—to my profound astonishment—the three of them were standing by the quay again and gazing out into the ocean.

I took note that another boat was coming in, but paid it little heed at first. Instead, I went speeding toward the sergeant, clambered down and told him what I'd found.

He listened patiently, but shook his head.

"What you must have found was evidence of kids at play. No, this case—I'm afraid to say—reaches its conclusion with a sorry end."

He nodded at the approaching craft, which was closer now so I could make its details out. It was a motor launch with a strong chugging engine, painted a light shade of blue and with the words *Harbor Patrol* along its flank and with the city flag of Providence flapping at the stern. Another man in uniform was steering it, and his companion was standing over an uneven shape that was covered with a tarpaulin. Then I took in something else. A little rowing boat, its insides damp, was being towed behind the larger craft.

I glanced to my right and, as I had begun suspecting, one of the small boats which had been tethered there was gone.

"It seems Miss Ellen and her beau took it in their heads to go out on the water. Inexperienced as they were, their boat capsized. We haven't found her body yet, and with the kinds of currents round these parts perhaps we never might."

I tried to picture that entire scenario, but could see that it made little sense. Why take a ferry over to an island and then go out on the sea again? Except the patrol launch was heaving to, ropes being thrown across and tied. And when I stared down into it, I could see there was a shock of wet blond hair protruding out from underneath the edge of the canvas cloth.

McMannis climbed down and pulled the covering away. It was the same young man who I had looked at two days back.

v

I found myself being ignored beyond that point. The search was over—this was nothing but official business now. But, shocked and saddened as I was, I still hung around for a good long while.

A local doctor was called in—this fellow too had a creased and pallid face and a faraway look in his near colorless eyes—to certify the young man's death. The sergeant went to find a telephone, to convey news of this tragedy to the mainland.

For myself, I was still pretty unconvinced. That gorgeous young couple was captured in my mind's eye just as clearly as if I had seen them no more than an hour ago. And they'd been heading into the main body of the town, had shown no slightest interest in the rowing boats. Why turn around again ... why go out there? It did not add up and my head hurt.

"Let's wrap it up, boys!" McMannis was shouting as he ambled back toward us.

And this was too much, the final straw. They were treating this whole disaster like it was of no consequence.

Slowly—with a helpless feeling that rendered me almost numb—I pedaled back toward the beach. And when I finally reached it, I studied all those prints again. Nothing more than kids at play? It honestly did not look like that.

The tracks leading up from the sea could clearly not be followed to their source. The ones emerging from the grasses, though? I went after them as best I could, trying to find out where they originated from. It was not easy; the sea-grasses were dense and the ground beneath them increasingly hard. I managed to track them for about eight yards but then they simply faded off.

Exasperation had me in its grip. I came to a halt and stood upright, breathing heavily, my hands on my hips. Then abruptly, in the corner of my eye, I caught sight of a flash of color. Was that pink? I strode across.

Lying upside-down among the tall dry reeds, half-closed and with some of its thin spokes bent, was the parasol I'd seen Helen carrying.

And when I bent to pick it up, I saw its metal stem was twisted almost to a right-angle.

CHAPTER SIX

A Scream

i

Everyone had vanished by the time that I got back again. The doctor had gone home and I had no idea which part of town he had come here from; the motor launch had disappeared and taken the policemen with it. My exasperation was increased threefold, I cycled home as quickly as I could, still clutching that parasol, and once there I snatched up my phone and asked the operator to connect me.

"Narragansett Reserve," came a woman's voice

I told her what this was about and what I'd found. But:

"No, it's been recorded as a drowning, sir."

"I've –"

"Parasols can blow away—believe me, sir, it happens all the time. This is now officially an accident, with no further detail required."

Her voice sounded dull and pitchless, and she seemed almost mesmeric in her inability to change her mind. But maybe that was down to the confined mentality that bureaucrats and lowlier officials often have. And it wasn't too much longer before she apologized and then hung up on me.

I spent the entire afternoon just gazing at that pink umbrella, remembering the lovely face beneath it, and I got no writing done at all.

ii

There! Following the instructions in the cookbook I had bought, I'd managed to make myself an omelet. It was a decidedly odd shape and dark brown along one edge, but at least it was a start. Give me a few weeks and I'd transform myself into Auguste Escoffier.

But I knew what I was really doing—trying to divert myself a little and cheer myself up, since I'd been in a gloomy and depressive mood the whole remainder of this day. Every time I blinked I could see flashes of blond and red hair. How delightful they had been and how besotted with each other.

The light was failing at my windows as it always did about this hour, that unearthly silence which accompanied it descending like a heavy fog. Once that I had finished up my meal, I tried to think what else I ought to do. Play another disc? But I was almost in a state of mourning, and listening to some lively jazz was not something I much felt in the mood for now.

Maybe I could listen to some news instead, the business of the outside world distracting me? Let's face it, I had gotten badly out-of-touch, and maybe the reception had cleared up. So I crossed to the wireless and switched it on, except I wasn't even getting normal static by this stage. Instead of that, there was a high-pitched whining noise which fluctuated up and down, rising at times to such an intense squealing that it almost made me flinch.

And beneath that awful sound, I thought that I could hear some type of moaning voice. It was there in any which direction that I took the dial, so I couldn't tell where it was coming from. A low deep monotone that wasn't speaking English and which barely sounded as if it was being issued from a human throat.

"Ph'nglui mglw'nafh," was what I thought I heard. *"Wgah'nagl fhtagn."*

And what kind of language was that? I tried to lose it, moving the dial swiftly, but it wouldn't go away. Angry and confused, I switched the wireless off.

But immediately after I had done that, I heard a different kind of noise. A bicycle other than my own, whizzing past on the lane outside. And then I heard another one.

Ever since I'd moved into this place, I had not seen or heard a single passer-by. But now there appeared to be two of them, and I had to wonder what their destination was. I went to my front windowpane, but both the riders were already gone.

A sudden distant clopping started up. And within a minute more, a horse and cart hove into view, not the taxicab which had first brought me here but a larger carriage with four wheels and with its interior covered up. I could make out the faint outline of the driver at the reins but of the people inside I could catch no view. The horse kept trotting and the vehicle moved on. I stepped onto my porch and watched it being swallowed by the deepening night.

There were other sounds emerging now from further down the lane, other horses headed up this way, most probably from Marinsberg, although I knew by this time that there were more houses out beyond the fringes of the town. But what was going on this evening that had made this soporific place quite suddenly come alive this way?

The hooves drew closer but then stopped a distance from my place. At the poetess's home, perhaps? Such was the bend in the dusty lane though, I could not be sure, and at a loss for what to do I just went back inside.

Whatever might be happening, it didn't seem to involve me. Till fairly recently, I'd always been a sociable man, so that did nothing to improve my mood. My depression grew worse and was accompanied by an isolated feeling I had rarely known. I needed to close my mind to all of this, and so I chose one of the novels I had brought with me—*Main Street* by Sinclair Lewis—sat down on my couch and tried to lose myself in it.

It was some fifteen minutes later when a faint hubbub of voices started up. Curious, I set the book aside and went to my back door, and it was definitely coming from the Gorsting residence. The hubbub gradually increased in pitch but there was nothing strange in that, people having to talk ever louder to make themselves heard above the general throng, just like every party that I'd ever hung around.

But then there was a swift loud whoop which made me stiffen in my shoes. And then another, sharper one, and those were followed up by something like a feral growl. So what in God's name were these people doing? I could hear a woman start to shout and I was pretty sure it was the poetess, and so I headed up to my bedroom where I could take a better look.

Due to the intervening privets, I could not see the gardens and could not make out the crowd. Except the balcony was fully lit, the French windows spread wide behind it. And at the parapet and leaning dangerously over it was the unmistakably tall figure of this evening's hostess.

She was waving both her arms and tossing her long hair and yelling down at the assembly below, but she was so far distant that I only caught brief snatches of her words.

"Soon!" I thought I heard. "Won't have long to wait!"

"Awoken and she sees us now!"

And then an even longer phrase, bellowed so hard that I could make it out in full.

"The stars are on their proper course! They'll be aligned correctly in a few more months!"

So maybe she was back on her astronomy kick, though what it had to do with all the other people down there was a puzzle to my way of thinking.

Here's the really strange thing, though. Every time she let loose a pronouncement, it was greeted with delight by the throng below. More whoops and shrieks, and even some manner of ululating warbling.

Anastasia straightened up at last and turned away, disappearing back into her house, so I presumed that she was going down the stairs to mingle with the people there. Except that 'mingle' is a polite word, and what came next was far from that.

Noises that were violent began crashing round my ears, abrupt shapeless yells and howls, and at one point a cacophony of snarling like some kind of brawl had broken out. I knew she threw wild parties, but had not expected anything like this; it was like listening to wild animals and not people at all. And it went on and on until my blood ran cold. What kind of whoopee-juice were these guys on?

I was breathing very shallowly by now. And I was thinking seriously of picking up the phone again and getting put through to whatever authorities might be presiding on this isle ...

When the dreadful racket—without any preamble—completely stopped, dying away to nothingness.

Which itself was cut across by a soft mechanical whirring, as of cogs and gears. Then there was a scraping sound, metal rasping gently against metal. And a peculiar bright light started flooding up.

iii

I'd seen it before, on the first night I was here, but this was not merely a flash. It was neither blue nor green but a peculiar mix of both. And it was not an even shade but fluctuated, pulsed, seemed to ripple in the way seawater does. What was producing it I could not guess, but it spread out across the hidden gardens, lighting up the hedges and the dark back wall, and it then rose against the blue-black sky like it was challenging the very stars.

Anastasia Gorsting's voice rang out again, loudly and stridently. But it was just two words this time, and both of them extremely odd.

The first seemed to be 'Zulu.' Had I even heard that right? Why would she think to shout out the name of some African tribe?

But the second word was more confounding, and appeared to be a part of that bizarre diatribe I had listened to on my radio.

'Fhtagn. '

What was that honestly? Fourteen? For time? It made no tiniest grain of sense. But Anastasia shouted out those two words several times.

And then I thought I could hear something else … another female voice, but far softer and higher-pitched. The voice, it seemed, of a much younger woman. And I could not grasp what she was saying, but her tone seemed to be desperate and almost trembling. Was she pleading, and if so for what?

There was a sudden scream next second, cutting through the darkness like a knife. Whether it was out of pain or fear I could not tell, but it was definitely real enough. It rushed at me, then warbled to a halt.

And my numbness of before was gone. Something terrible was happening out there. I was charging down the stairs before I knew it, bursting out into the warm night air and running down the lane toward the Gorsting house.

iv

With only the light of a quarter moon to guide me, I was in a world of shadow now, nothing substantial to be seen but only shades of gray and black. There were no lights on in the houses that I passed. The trees beside the lane seemed like tall pillars of gloominess that gradually merged with the night sky, and the surrounding flattened landscape seemed to jog and jerk with every frantic step I took.

The house started coming into view again. Lit up fully as it was, it formed a massively dense black presence against the backdrop of the night-bound countryside, and the yellow of its windows only served to emphasize that.

Some larger gates were open in the fence by now, and parked in the forecourt were a good number of carriages—each one tethered to a bedraggled-looking horse—and numerous bicycles as well. So how many of the islanders were attending this shindig?

There was no sound coming from the back at all by this stage, and that peculiar blue-green light had apparently been turned off. I started trying to pick my way between the carriages, but got a pretty startling result.

The horses all began to shriek and rear up, with their eyes so wide that they were mostly white and pale foam dripping from their lips. These were pathetic creatures, I could see, undernourished and ill-groomed and teetering on the verge of panic. The stench of their sweat filled the air. They seemed to my mind far more like captive beings than typical domestic steeds.

But it was not their welfare I was here about, so I ducked past their lashing hooves and made it up the porch to the front door.

And I yanked on the bell-pull hard, my shoulders straining and my heart on fire. And after what seemed an age, I found myself confronted with that butler once again.

"Mr. Sinclair?"

"What the *hell* is going on in here?"

Cuesto's gaze met directly with mine, but otherwise his features did not shift a fraction.

"Going *on*, sir?"

"Don't play dumb with me!" I yelled. "Let me through—I need to see what's happening!"

When that demand got no response, my anxious urgency rose to such a pitch I fully lost control of my own actions. And I tried to push the man out of the way, setting both my palms against his chest and shoving at him angrily.

I had a good six inches over him, and when I'd lived in Boston I'd played sports and exercised, but I still didn't get the appropriate result. It was like trying to move a solid wall or, more accurately, a hill of bricks. His body seemed to have a kind of inner strength that had more to do with solid mass and density than any muscular power, like he was deeply rooted to the ground. I couldn't budge him one small inch.

"*Mr. Sinclair!*" came a furious voice from the far end of the lobby.

I could see Anastasia Gorsting hurrying toward me now. Or maybe I should say that she was 'storming,' since her stride was staccato and her face was twisted up with rage. She had on a flowing floor-length dress this time in some kind of pearlescent green, the train of which was sweeping across the marble tiles. In one hand she had a cigarette and in the other was a half-filled glass, and her eyebrows were raised imperiously.

Off behind her, some rear doors were opened wide and several of her guests were peering through. And they looked to me like regular men and women, in smart suits and fancy frocks. I glanced across briefly at them and couldn't get it through my head how people such as these folks could have made those noises that I'd heard.

But I was left with little time to dwell on that, because the poetess came to a violent halt and glared at me across her butler's shoulder.

"Seriously, you are manhandling the help? Apologize to Cuesto, right away!"

I was still far too worked up, however, to contemplate playing that game.

"Someone screamed! A woman, I am sure! I heard it clearly and demand to know what's happening to her!"

And Gorsting slackened off a little once I'd told her that, her fury dissipating just a touch so that the angle of her shoulders dropped and her features softened slightly.

"One of my much younger guests," she finally conceded, "became overexcited. Too much drink and too much liveliness, and unfortunately she had a fit. Another of my guests here is a doctor—he's attending to her now and assures me she will be okay. But she needs rest and quiet, Mr. Sinclair, not frantic neighbors bursting through."

Okay, that sounded fairly reasonable. I'd seen gals getting dizzy or much worse than that at big loud parties previously.

"But what is this whole bash?" I tried.

"A private gathering for all the friends I've made and all of the like-minded souls since I first arrived here. We come together underneath the stars and celebrate the beauty of the Cosmos. And we do that fervently, with high emotion, letting our true natures loose."

Only the islanders I'd met so far had mostly seemed defined by 'dull,' so what could have turned that around?

Her guests had vanished from the opening at the back. All that I could see was a section of the gardens, delicately lit up with a gentle amber glow. But that had not been the case earlier.

"What was that strange light?" I asked.

"A new sort of artwork I'm experimenting with, color not on canvas but on the night air instead."

And then she paused and rearranged her thoughts.

"But maybe I've been rude as well. I overlooked inviting you. So, would you like to come on in?"

Except that, after everything I'd heard, after all those frightening snarls and shrieks, I was not sure I had the stomach for it, however graciously the invitation might be put.

I stared past the woman into the first floor interior. And once again, my sense of perspective seemed to shift, so that the walls and floor looked like they were at unusual angles to each other, the ceiling far too low, the winding stairs at an oblique tilt. Giddiness began to overtake me, only maybe I was simply too worked up, the blood in my veins too hot. When I jerked my gaze away, my sense of balance came immediately back. So I steadied myself and held my ground.

"No thanks, but I think I'll pass on that. Sounds to me like the party's over anyway."

And I was about to start turning away when another thought occurred to me.

"I heard a couple of the things that you were shouting from the balcony."

"Yes?"

"Who woke up? Who's watching us?"

The woman grinned, displaying all her teeth.

"Just another poem I've been working on. I often like to perform some selections from them to my guests."

Which sounded to me like a 'check' and 'mate.' She had given me a fairly plausible answer to every single question I had asked. Her face was entirely calm, but I could see a gleam of triumph in her one good eye.

And the Sinclair bloodline has one inherited quality ... we always know when we are being dunned. And that was what this felt like to the inner instincts that I had.

What could I do about it, though? All that I could manage was to shrug.

"Okay, then. Until we meet again?"

"I'm sure we shall, Mr. Sinclair. I'm pretty certain that we shall become important to each other in some way."

And I couldn't understand, not for the life of me, what she might be alluding to, but with those words she turned briskly away. And her butler began closing the front door again.

Just before the latch clicked shut, though, I managed to catch yet another glimpse of someone high up on the stairs, crouching down and peering at me from between the railings of the bannister. It was the same young woman I had spotted briefly on the first occasion I'd been here—she had on a floaty white dress and looked very delicately-built. But then the door slid firmly into place, leaving me with nothing but to back away.

I went past the horses that were still extremely nervous, but I stopped again at the front gate. And realized there was still somebody watching me.

On the roof of the house's left-hand wing, I could just about make out a figure hunched down on all fours, so enfolded in shadow he was barely visible. Except that he looked almost as small as a child, and his protruding forehead seemed to bulge.

This was the same deformed homunculus I had encountered on the ferry coming over here. And what was a creature like this even doing at such a gathering?

He seemed to get the fact he had been spotted. And, without lifting any higher, he turned himself around and scuttled out of sight.

Once that I was sure he was completely gone, I made my way back slowly to my own small house, my mind full of unease and doubt and plagued by the unhappy feeling that I was still being watched.

CHAPTER SEVEN
THE GIRL IN WHITE

i

I did not sleep well that night and was in a dull cold mood for most of the next day. And the weather had begun to match the state that I was in. Even in July, the climate off of the north-east coastline can quite unexpectedly, abruptly change. A strong easterly wind had blown in overnight, bringing with it a huge mass of cloud, so that the landscape all around my house looked bled of color and washed-out.

I tried to write for well over an hour, but found I could not force myself to concentrate. And so, frustration setting in, I decided to go out on another lengthy ride.

I headed away from Marinsberg this time. I'd found a map inside a kitchen drawer back at the house, and studying it I had discerned that, unlike Martha's Vineyard, there were no more towns on this large island, only hamlets and then individual homes. But I wanted to take a good look at them and get some idea what the people out there were about.

Everywhere I traveled to was absolutely flat. The wind whistled around me, tugging at my hair and clothes, but save for the brisk whirr of my bike's gears it was the only sound that I could hear. Occasionally, an isolated house would appear in the distance, but with no least sign of activity around it. And that was a pattern that I found repeated constantly. This whole place seemed to be asleep, and I couldn't help but wonder why that was.

At long last, I reached a section of the shoreline totally composed of broad flat rock, and I walked out across it till I found a ridge where I sat down. And gazing out to sea—which was a dull gray too, and filled with choppy waves by now—I tried to get my head around all those questions that were still troubling me.

Zulu fhtagn? What was that? Perhaps the poetess had begun experimenting not simply with colored light but, as she had hinted when I'd first met her, with language too, in the matter of Gertrude Stein.

But there were other facts that equally concerned me. Did young women in the grip of a seizure scream as loud and hard as that? I was no doctor and I wasn't sure.

What bothered me beyond that point, and truly so, was this. Anastasia's guests last night had obviously been local people. And yet, ever since I'd first arrived, I'd barely seen a faint suggestion of them. They almost always remained in their homes and out of sight, like they were hiding from the world.

How could it be possible that such secretive types could without any warning alter their demeanor in the furious way that I had heard last night? That snarling and those shrieks and yells. Their wild approval of Miss Gorsting's words. It was almost like this was an island full of maniacs, with not one personality but two. And what could have inspired that massive shift in their behavior?

I did not know and could not figure the conundrum out, however hard I set my thoughts to it. My furrowed brow was almost hurting now, my mind was under so much stress. And so I decided to drop the matter, simply take some small pleasure in being where I was. I lit a fresh cigar and watched the smoke billow away from me.

The waves were thumping on the rocks, flecks of brine hitting my face, except I didn't care and simply let that happen. Far out on the surface of the sea, a large yacht was tacking hard—it looked to be at least a mile away. And the coastline of the mainland was a misty blur that looked like nothing more than low cloud, barely real.

Well, Sinclair, I told myself, *you've now got all the solitude you'll ever want.* But when not writing, what exactly was I going to do with it?

Perhaps it might be a good, even a sensible idea, to let some of my people from back home know where I had departed to and how I could be reached. My house had more than one bedchamber, after all, and so I could play host to some guests if that circumstance arose.

I was about to stand up again when my gaze fell on something that was rather odd. Far out on the ocean, I could make out a broad area of water where the thrashing waves had died down noticeably, as if something very large had moved up underneath them and was baffling their natural force.

For the briefest moment, I believed that I could detect something on the move out there—a swift sharp flicker like a moving limb. It couldn't possibly be that, though. What was it really, just a streak of foam? It disappeared almost immediately, and beyond that point the dull reflective surface revealed nothing.

But with Block Island Sound off to the west of here and Vineyard Sound off to the east, this stretch of ocean had to be subject to vagaries of current that were often strange. Little wonder that you sometimes saw peculiar configurations of the tide like this. I climbed back on my bicycle and wheeled away.

And I *did* start writing when I got back home. I banged away at it for practically two hours, but all that I wound up with at the end of all that work were characters who were depressive and who spoke in clipped and muted tones. And this book was supposed to be a comedy in part, so I tore the sheets of paper up and binned them all.

Supper this evening was a can of stew—I'd gotten no further with the cookbook that I'd bought. And I was just finishing up when I heard something that was entirely unexpected.

Fingernails it sounded like, tapping delicately on the small glass pane in my front door. I thought at first I was imagining it … but no, the brief sharp rattle came again. I had a caller, and I'd never been expecting that, and I was so surprised I almost jumped.

Calming myself down, I brushed my shirt-front flat, ran two fingers through my hair, then went to find out who was standing on my porch.

It was the same young woman I had twice glimpsed at the Gorsting house.

ii

The light, which had been dull all day, was starting to fade earlier than was usual and my covered porch was full of darkened shade. In which she stood out like a jewel, so pale her clothing and complexion were.

Discounting her heels, she stood at little more than five foot three and was so extremely slender that her waist was tiny and her narrow limbs looked almost brittle. She had on a knee-length dress composed of white delicate lace and with the shoulders bare and low-cut at the front. Black hair, tousled, tumbled down her back. But the real thing was I could not properly see her face, since her head was lowered and she did not lift it, not even when I moved myself directly in front of her. All she did was intertwine her fingers like some nervous schoolgirl waiting for her teacher to speak.

A delicate and fragile vision then. And how old? It was hard to tell.

"Yes?" I enquired of her.

And perhaps I did that a little too sharply. I was still perplexed as to why she had come here, after all. Her head twitched but still stayed low. And then she murmured something I could barely hear.

I leaned in closer.

"What was that?"

"You seem nice," she told me in a tiny voice.

My puzzlement, already strong, was beginning to become intense.

"And you can tell that how? From high up on the stairs?"

"When that girl screamed, you came to help. She was new—I'd not seen her before. Except you tried to force your way inside, you were so intent on discovering what was wrong. You care about other people, sir. So it is my belief that you are nice."

All of which was relayed in a low, breathy whisper, more an exhalation than a proper set of words. And the way she phrased them ... more in the style of a Victorian woman than a modern girl. I noticed she was shivering gently, fine hairs standing up on her forearms. But I still had no idea what she was doing here.

"Excuse me," I asked again, "but who exactly are you?"

And her face came up at last. An almost perfect oval as I'd believed earlier on, the nose small, as were the ears, a slight pink blush across her cheeks. And her lips, pressed together, were the color of a rose. A quite beautiful face, in fact, although the eyes were the most striking feature. They were huge and glowed a shade of green I'd only once ever seen.

"I'm Katia Gorsting," she told me in that same hushed voice. "Anastasia Gorsting's daughter."

iii

Anastasia Gorsting's *what?* I felt absolutely thunderstruck.

Never once, in all of the news columns I had read about the poetess, had there been the briefest mention of a child. Never once had she been photographed with such. The rumor mill had never alluded to it, and as far as I was aware she'd never entered into any marriage vow.

Yet here was this pale, slim and pretty phantom, seriously claiming to be of her bloodline, and clearly too guileless and innocent to manage such a massive lie. But if she was really who she was claiming to be, then how should I respond to that?

"If that's so then I'm pleased to meet you. But what are you doing here?"

"You seem nice," she said again.

"Your point being?"

"Well … I know no one else who is."

I felt my eyes widening when she told me that. It was a type of outright statement I had never heard before. Back at the house, did she mean? Was she surrounded every day by people that she did not like? That would certainly explain the cowed and subdued way that she presented herself.

"Seriously?" I tried. "There must be someone?"

Katia gave her head a little shake.

"What's the deal here? Are you afraid for your safety?"

"Not that really, no. Mostly I'm just miserable and tired."

"You'd better come on in, then," I told her carefully, and I edged back to let her through.

Her first couple of steps were extremely timid, and she glanced around my living room as though she was suspecting it might be a spring-trap that could suddenly snap shut around her. But then she decided that was not the case, and she headed quickly for my couch. She sat down on it in the same way that a bird might perch, then drew her heels up after her without so much as bothering to remove her shoes. And she took a longer look at the dull brown room, very curiously this time around, as though she was astonished that the inside of another person's home was rather different to her own.

I watched her closely that first minute and then sat down myself in an armchair opposite, waiting for her to shift her focus back to me. And I waited for quite a while. What was this young lady's deal?

"Aren't you going to ask me what my name is, Katia?"

Her green gaze fixed on me an instant but then darted away again.

"You're Mr. Sinclair. I heard my mother call it out."

"It's Jackson," I corrected her, "except most people call me Jay."

"Like the bird?"

"Yes."

"That's nice. I wish I had a name like that."

"Does your mother know you're here?"

"She doesn't care. She's always acted like I don't exist. The Chinese maid looks after me, but she is always bad-tempered and cruel."

"And how old are you, if I might ask?"

"I turned eighteen last month, or so I'm told."

"No birthday party? Presents?"

"No."

"But what else do you do? Do you still go to school?"

Her attention had fastened on the ceiling now—she'd spotted a cobweb up there and she didn't even try to answer me.

I asked her: "What is it that you're expecting, coming here?"

"I *hate* the way I'm forced to live. And so I thought I'd try it here instead, where I'd feel comfortable, since you seem nice."

It occured to me—relating this whole conversation—I am making her sound stupid and weak-minded, but I got the strongest sense she was not that. Rather that her consciousness had come detached somehow and it was floating freely like a mayfly on the breeze. If what she'd said about her mom was true—and having met the elder Gorsting twice, I had no cause to doubt it—then this Katia was living the strange life of an abandoned waif, almost like an orphan, save that her one parent was not even dead.

Gradually, by slow degrees, I got more details of her existence from her. She'd never been to school at all but had been taught to read, and she'd learnt everything she knew from books. She had no friends and did not seem entirely sure what such types of people were. When she'd had to venture out, she had been forced to do so in disguise, with much use of wide-brimmed hats and limousines with darkly-tinted windows.

So her existence had been kept an impenetrable secret, Gorsting hiding from the entire world the fact that she had given birth. But why? I couldn't even *start* to understand it.

"Were you at the party last night?"

The next shake of her head was emphatically brisk.

"They always scare me, they're so loud. And that one was the loudest yet."

"So you were …?"

"On the stairs and listening."

"And do you usually end up there?"

She looked slightly awkward as her chin went up and down.

And that was when I got the clearest impression of her I'd received so far. Both the times I'd seen her, she'd been on the stairs. Except the plain fact is that people who are hiding usually do so in some kind of room, and a flight of steps is not nearly the same thing as that. This was a young woman who appeared to exist in the empty spaces and the hollow gaps between what you and I would call normality, somebody who only lived a fraction of a normal life. I was starting to feel truly sorry for her, but there was one more query that I felt the need to put.

"Did you see what happened to the girl who screamed?"

"I only heard her, nothing more."

"And when the party finished up?"

"She must have left with all the other guests."

It was almost fully dark by now, silence clamping round the house again. I glanced over at my window, then at my wristwatch.

"It's getting quite late, Katia. So maybe I should walk you home."

For the first time since she had arrived here, her eyes battened on my own and then began to noticeably dampen.

"I'm so very unhappy back there, I cannot even sleep for very long."

"No?"

"It would be so nice if I could manage that. And so … can I stop here tonight?"

Was she kidding me? But obviously not.

"Nobody will notice that you're gone?"

"Just the maid, and she hates me."

I'd already been thinking of taking in some house-guests, except that this was not what I had had in mind. But what the hell … the poor damned kid. If it made her happier, I saw no reason why she shouldn't stay. I showed her up to one of my spare rooms, found some bed linen and even gave her one of my white shirts to sleep in.

Jackson Maynard Sampson Sinclair, a bachelor of long standing, alone in a house in the middle of plain nowhere with a teenaged cutie underneath his roof. Eyebrows would be raised in Boston, but I was no longer there and I could make up my own rules.

Returning to the kitchen, I poured myself a shot. And stepping through into the living room again, I heard the floorboards creaking overhead, Katia moving round up there. And without even meaning to, I visualized her slipping off that lacy dress.

I've played the field—don't get me wrong. I'd earned myself, back where I used to live, a solid reputation as a ladies' man. And ever since the Twenties had begun to roar that whole business had gotten even more involved. *Flappers welcome*, a sign ought to read over my bedroom door. But Katia was so slight and frail, with a mentality much younger than she really was. And forlorn with it, a benighted soul, and so my conscience wouldn't let me go that route. The Garden of Earthly Delights was not a place where she belonged.

I was still telling myself that when my whole sense of perspective shifted once again, the walls of this room appearing to tilt. I was not overtired and hadn't drunk too much and could not figure what was causing this. In an attempt to clear my vision up, I clamped my eyes briefly shut.

Bubbles rose. A thick tentacle writhed. And everything was tinted green.

A partial repeat of that dream I'd had. But what had brought it back?

When my eyes opened again, my hand had dropped and I'd spilled half my drink. Goddammit, what was wrong with me? I downed the rest then wiped my fingers clean. It was now absolutely quiet upstairs, with not another sound from Katia's room, but I was still aware that she was there.

Ever since I'd moved in here, with little but my work to distract me, I'd been turning in much earlier than I used to do. And perhaps that was the wise course now, since drinking more could only lead to trouble. I headed quietly up to my bedroom, closed the door firmly behind me, stripped down to my boxers and switched off the light. And once down, I turned my back to the wall past which Katia was lying and I tried to pretend that she was not there.

I have to admit that was hard.

iv

Keeping her hidden, and for eighteen years as well. Did her ego-driven mother think a daughter would draw the public's gaze away from her? And damage her wild reputation equally? But it seemed insane behavior, for chrissake!

I kept on remembering something else that Katia had told me, though. *'She was new—I'd not seen her before.'* And she had been talking about that woman who had screamed, but who could be a new face here on Sauquill, since the visitors who came here did not stay. Perhaps she simply meant a local she had not encountered earlier on. Yes, I reassured myself, that had to be the case. I grunted gently and then tried to sleep.

A massive doorway slid open obliquely and a face began emerging, half-covered with twisting feelers.

My gaze snapped back open, and when I tried to shut my eyes a second time I got precisely the same result, that weird vision coming to me again. So, perplexed to the point of sheer annoyance, I lay there in the dark with my lids wide open.

From back behind me came the softest rasp of wood on carpet, and I stiffened and then held myself completely still. Somebody was opening my bedroom door, and there was just one person it could be.

"Jay?" came her soft, plaintive voice.

For the love of God, what did she think that she was doing?

"I'm still nervous and I cannot get to sleep."

"And?"

"Can I get into bed with you?"

I practically exploded, but was careful not to turn around.

"What is this—do you seriously think that you're some little kid? You're an almost full-grown woman and of marriageable age!"

She paused a short while, and then:

"I'll be very quiet," she said.

And before I could do anything to stop it, she had clambered in and she was lying there right next to me. I forced myself to not respond, my whole frame rigid by this stage.

"Night-night, Jay," I heard her murmur.

"Yuh," I managed to respond, though I did that through gritted teeth.

I pressed my eyelids shut again.

And could see just one tentacle this time, and it was beginning to straighten out.

I could smell her hair and the perfume of her skin. And the warmth from her body seemed to reach my naked back. No more than a kid, less than half my age. I kept reminding myself that.

The tentacle—in the darkness in my skull—was now completely straight. And another moved toward it and then curled around.

Her warmth was being matched by the heat under my skin. The smell of her was overpowering, and I could no longer help myself. In one swift motion I rolled over, half afraid that she would scream.

But instead she smiled in the faint moonlight that was shining through my bedroom window, folded her hands across my shoulders and accepted me.

CHAPTER EIGHT

BRINK

i

S he had vanished altogether by the time that I awoke, my white shirt lying on the floor and all her clothing gone from the spare room. The bad weather had passed and clear unsullied sunlight was now streaming in.

I found myself moving slowly and wearily about the house, beset by the uncomfortable feeling I had made some kind of very bad mistake. It hadn't even been good lovemaking, just a brisk and urgent coupling.

She had been no more than a teenager, and with the mindset of an even younger girl. *Holy hell, Sinclair. You must be getting old if you have started giving in to appetites like that.* I kept on trying to tell myself that it was she who'd crawled into my bed. But what had all those visions of those writhing feelers been about?

I expected her to come back in the next few days, but Katia did not reappear. I went riding past her house and she was nowhere to be seen. And so that was the end of that, apparently. Either she was crazier than I'd first thought or her innocent naivety was just an act and she was just as footloose as her mom.

I decided to forget the entire matter and tried to continue with my life at a steady and a measured pace. I wrote. I explored some more. I fried a fillet of fish with some success. I also got on the phone and told a few friends I'd be pleased to see them.

And who should turn up at my door, five days later and completely unannounced? Of all people, smiling chirpy Brinkley Breslaw, quite a few years junior to me and sole heir to the Breslaw Fabrics fortune.

Don't misunderstand me—Brink's okay. He's always happy, which is a good thing. But that happiness, to put it bluntly, derives from the fact he's not too bright, thinks no deep thoughts and therefore is not troubled by them.

"What ho, sport!" he grinned at me.

Which was his usual greeting and I nodded back a little flatly. Tall and thin as the proverbial beanpole, he had on pale beige attire, a flat cap and his usual plus-fours.

"Any room for another crew member on this brand-new ship of yours?"

"It's a house, Brink, not a ship."

"I meant that as a meta what-not."

I think he was referring to a metaphor.

I ushered him in all the same. He had a rather large valise with him. But he insisted, and immediately too, on looking round the entire place, his step eager as he headed up the stairs.

"Rather different from your place on Beacon Hill, eh? Rather rustic, I might say. You're here alone?"

"More or less. Where's Midge?" I asked.

Midge Ellmans being his fiancée of the past three years, a rather pushy round-faced girl no cleverer than Brinkley was. Neither of them seemed to understand that marriage ought to follow after the presentation of an engagement ring.

"She's on St. Lucia with her folks. And I was feeling lonesome, which is why I'm here."

He studied the watch which he had pulled out from his waistcoat pocket.

"Time for a late lunch, I'd say. Where's best for that?"

"There's nothing like that around here."

"Not even a coffee shop?"

"Not even a hot dog stand."

"But honestly," Brink asked, aghast, "what kind of wretched place is this?"

"I'm still trying to figure that one out."

ii

But he was so irrepressibly jolly he could actually be fairly decent company if you contrived to keep the conversation light. I brewed us some coffee and we hung around the porch. He brought me up to speed with Boston gossip and the comings and goings at the Somerset Club. I told him most of what I had been doing, even showing him the little sheaf of pages I had typed.

"Oh, good Lord, but I could never manage this. I'm awash with admiration—you're an artist now!"

We elected to go out for a walk, not sticking to the lane but cutting across the open fields in the direction of the coastline.

"What you really need, sport, in this setting is a dog."

But I had still not seen or even heard one the entire time I'd been here.

We finally reached a pebbled stretch of shore. The July sun was burning brightly and its yellow was reflected on the crests of waves and, unlike earlier, you could see the mainland clearly now, the low buildings of Narragansett looking like some finely-detailed watercolor.

"Just smell that air!" my companion beamed, and he drew in a deep lungful of it. "Lord, but what a splendid view!"

But then he took on a rather thoughtful look, which was highly unusual for him. I watched as his forehead creased and his gaze lost a touch of its cheerful clarity.

"That big dark ugly house along the lane? I saw it on the way to yours. Who on earth would live in such a place?"

I told him and then watched him as his long jaw dropped.

"Her? You're kidding me. But seriously?" He peered back in the direction we had come. "Really truly her? But have you met her yet?"

"Twice, in fact."

"And what was she like, sport? Was she almost naked? Was she foaming at the mouth?"

We strolled gently along the tideline while I told him much of what I had found out. I made little mention of that raucous gathering though, and did not speak of Katia at all. Maybe I was respecting her privacy, or perhaps I felt awkward about what had happened that strange night.

"Golly!" was my guest's response. "She sounds scary, and the opposite of nice."

We started heading back across the fields again.

"D'you suppose it's true?" Brink asked me suddenly. "Those parties that she used to throw?"

"Most rumors have some basis in the truth."

"And right next door to decent people? I'm not sure Midge would approve of that at all."

We were almost home and beginning to cross the lane when a new sight on my porch made me slow right down.

Set beneath the wicker chairs this time, there were two large bottles of what looked to be red wine. And when I picked one up, the label told me it was Chateau Cartier, the poetess's favorite brew.

I'd not received this kind of gift before, but that seemed to have changed because I had a house-guest by this juncture. So it seemed that absolutely nothing happened here without Miss Gorsting finding out.

iii

Supper was a princely meal of drumsticks of steamed chicken—Midge had shown Brink how to cook that way, using just a colander with a big lid atop it—canned baked beans and fine Bordeaux. Afterwards we found a half-filled oil lamp and we sat out on the porch and played gin rummy for ten cents a point, and I managed to win twenty-seven bucks off him.

The light was turning ever dimmer, and the darkness closed around us like a slowly-clenching fist.

"It's awfully quiet," Brink remarked. "Refreshing in its own strange way."

But not long after that, he started yawning.

"All of this sea air, I guess."

I showed him up to the same room I had put Katia in. And once he was settled, I headed back downstairs, poured myself a whisky and resumed my reading of the Sinclair Lewis book.

It was almost midnight by the time that I was done. I started switching off the downstairs lights, but then noticed something I had not before. There was another kind of light, a tinted one, filtering in through my back windows. So I went through to the kitchen and looked out.

That peculiar bluish-greenish glow was emanating from the grounds behind Miss Gorsting's house again. Pulsing, fluctuating, rippling like a tidal pool. Only that it seemed more concentrated now—it rose into the air in an almost-solid column, far higher than it had before. But there seemed to be no gathering this time, no shrieks or yells or mindless braying. And so maybe she was genuinely experimenting with a brand-new form of art.

And yet ... it didn't really look like that to my suspicious gaze. It looked rather more to me like some manner of signal or beacon. For the benefit of who or what?

There was no telling what was really going on in the mind of my exotic neighbor, so I pushed it out of my head and I climbed the stairs. Brink's door was slightly ajar but with the gap unlit, and so he had to be asleep by now, except I could still hear his voice.

A low shapeless mumbling, so he was talking in his sleep. I'd never realized he was prone to that, and could not tell what he was trying to say.

Then he rolled over—I could hear the bedsprings creak—and uttered three syllables clearly.

"R'lyeh."

Lost in dreaming as he had to be, he was muttering nothing but sheer formless nonsense. I headed for my own bedroom and gave it no more thought.

iv

He was nowhere to be seen the next morning, though his case was still there in his room. Only I was not overly surprised by that. People who have simple and uncomplicated ways of thinking generally arrange their lives around some kind of strict routine, and that often includes early rising. It is only we sophisticates who stay up late and oversleep and have no structure to their day.

I supposed he must have gone out for a solitary walk. It was another sunny day, and so why not? I fixed myself some fresh coffee and had a go at making some French toast.

And I was hunting for the cinnamon when Brink walked in.

Not a word from him. Not 'Morning, Jay' or 'What a pleasant day' or 'That smells good.'

All he did was stare at me, and his gaze appeared to have gone blank again.

"You okay?" I asked him curiously.

I only favored him with a brief glance though, since I'd put too little butter in the pan and was afraid the bread was going to burn, and that held my attention for a while so that I didn't really notice what was going on.

I finally tipped the slices of toast onto the first plate that I could find and then looked at him with a small triumphant grin.

"Tuck in, feller. Help yourself."

But then my smile faded away, in most part because he wasn't smiling back. He no longer seemed his usual relaxed and happy self … far from it.

Gradually, the truth sank in. A massive change had overcome my guest, and one that had apparently happened overnight. He didn't even look as tall as normal, that down to the fact that his shoulders and his back were far more stooped than they had ever been. All the healthy pigment had now vanished from his face—it had taken on a grayish pallor and an unsettling shapelessness. I'd never seen Brink this way, his mouth downturned and his jowls loose.

It was his brownish-hazel eyes, however, that startled me the most. The twinkle and the cheeriness were gone from them; they seemed as unreflective as the pebbles on the beach where we had walked. Or maybe that was not quite correct and they were reflecting inwardly instead, and I had almost never known the guy do that.

He had, in short, a haunted look, like he had not fully awoken from that dream he'd had and was sleepwalking in the clear daylight.

"What's eating you, Brink?" I asked.

"I'm sorry, but I cannot stay."

"You're going back to Boston?"

"No."

I waited for him to explain.

"I went out for a walk at dawn."

"I got that, sure. But what of it?"

"I ran into that poetess, out on a constitutional herself."

Which was a new one on me. I'd only ever seen her in her house and had been unaware she went out past its gates.

"You never told me that she had a daughter, Jay."

At which point, I stiffened up.

"A pretty lass but rather shy. But as for Anastasia herself … we got to talking, quite a lot, and I found her absolutely fascinating."

"Honestly?"

"She opened up my mind in, oh, so many ways. The insignificance of mortal man. The possibility some higher purpose might exist. The chance that there could be some greater force—and I'm not talking of the Bible God—who might lead us to an elevated state of being."

"This a joke?" I blurted out

But when I stared into his largely-vacant eyes, I saw he was not kidding me.

"Oh, come on, Brink! She's nothing but a screwball with her head all full of mumbo-jumbo. Why exactly would a guy like you want anything to do with that? I'll find a bike for you and we can go off for a ride today."

That prospect, however, didn't seem to interest him. He was standing very still by now, almost like a dummy in a tailor's shop.

"She's invited me to stay a while."

In that monstrous house with its peculiar staff?

"She and I have so much to discuss."

And then he turned away from me and I could hear him heading up.

The French toast was forgotten by this stage. I'd known Brink a good few years and had never once believed that he was capable of this. Dwelling on philosophy and such? I couldn't have been more astonished if he'd informed me that he was going to the moon.

He was coming down now with his valise in his grasp, and didn't even throw a parting glance at me as he made for my door.

"You're not going to say goodbye?" I called out to his retreating back.

But I got not the tiniest response. He left the front door hanging open wide as he strode off toward the Gorsting residence. And I stepped out on the porch to watch him go.

"How long are you going to be there? What on earth do I tell Midge?"

And you'd have thought that the sound of his fiancée's name would slow him down a little bit. But Brink's attention did not shift, and before much longer he had disappeared around the broad curve in the lane.

V

It is at this point that I must pause in the recounting of these dire events, a reflection of my own coming to mind. It is in regard to the way that this Cthulhu influences us mere mortal beings, the hold that he has over us.

You've been with me for long enough that you know me to be an urbane type, with a perceptive mind and ready wit. But then there was Arnold Sewell, the proprietor of the news store, who struck me right away as quite an intelligent sort, with interests that went beyond the norm. Not to mention Sergeant McMannis, who I didn't get to know well till the very end of this, but who turned out to be a man of action and decisive thought.

I'm never going to claim people like us are wholly immune to Cthulhu's spell. That night with Katia, after all? We certainly can fall under his influence, only that we are not the targets that he goes for first. He principally fixes upon simpler minds, which explains why poor Brinkley got snared. As for the other islanders, their families had inhabited this place for countless generations, living uneventful lives, utterly unbothered by sophistication, and in that way their thought-processes had been gradually reduced to a bland mush. There was possibly inbreeding, and cross-breeding too … I will get to that final statement later on.

But the plain truth was that people such as these were like ripe apples hanging down from a low branch. And many years ago, Cthulhu had plucked them all and taken them for his own, and to be used in any way he wished.

His plans went far beyond that, though, and Anastasia was helping him. They wanted to turn the entire human race into a planet full of slaves.

CHAPTER NINE

ANOTHER FACE, ANOTHER 'PARTY'

i

I did not see or hear of Brink again for more than a whole week, although I thought about him often and looked out for him whenever I went past the Gorsting house. But there was no sign of his presence.

He was a full-grown man, I kept on telling myself, and so responsible for his own affairs. And, trying to stick to that idea, I did my level best to go back to living in the same way I had done before, only that didn't really work out well. His abrupt departure, and in such a style, had discomfited me badly and that showed itself in the uneven pattern of my work, that being brought on by my inability to concentrate.

The transformation that had overcome the guy had been so swift and utterly profound. I'd known Brink for practically a decade and had never seen him lost in introspection, never thought him *capable* of such a state. Where had the real Brink Breslaw gone and what kind of creature with the same face had replaced him?

My Remington did not clack much. I sat before it many times, but with my gaze directed into the thin air. What had Gorsting done to him?

I was in little doubt that it was she who was responsible for what had happened. Except that turned out to be only partly true. She, as it would later prove, was the channel for a vastly greater force.

Some people are taken by Cthulhu, yes. But others give themselves—and wholly willingly—to him and are his servitors and conduits in this world.

ii

We were almost into August now. The weather ought to have been heating up still further as we approached that glorious month. But Sauquill Island had now taken on a new and thoroughly displeasing aspect. It had begun attracting large batches of cloud, those and stiff cool breezes too, arriving from the north or east. Only that, from what I could make out, the rest of the Rhode Island coastline did not seem to be affected in such an unhappy way. I would cycle back down to the wooden quay or venture to that pebbled shore and, gazing at the mainland, I could see that it was brilliantly lit, sunlight picking out its distant features, like the countryside off there and this flat isle belonged to two completely different worlds.

This seemed to be a more peculiar place than I had ever been accounting for, the climate odd, the landscape strange, its inhabitants peculiar and elusive. And as for my infamous neighbor and the comings and the goings at her home …?

It was all a puzzle I could not resolve. But maybe it was that very conundrum that was stopping me from leaving here, a mystery my lively brain needed to discover the solution to. Every time that I considered going back to Boston, I came to the same conclusion, like my thought-processes were now traveling in a loop, although I didn't even notice they were doing that.

Anastasia Gorsting … what was she about? And how did she have such enormous influence on the people she had dealings with?

I was walking back one day from the pebbled shore, my head low and my thoughts tangled as I got closer to my house. And I was almost there when I picked out a sound I had not heard in quite a while, my telephone ringing in the living room.

Maybe it was Brink and he'd decided to come back. I took the porch steps in one leap, barged in through the front door and then snatched the handset up.

"That you, Jay?" asked a female voice.

And one that I immediately recognized. Crisp and rather snippy, with a definite school-marmish tone, this was none other than Midge Ellmans, Brink Breslaw's long-time fiancée, and she didn't even wait for me to answer.

"I understand that Brinky's with you. Would you kindly put him on?"

"I'm sorry, Midge, but he's not here, not anymore."

"And what in heaven's name does *that* mean?"

"He's moved in with a neighbor of mine down the road."

"Someone who he also knows?"

The timbre of her voice was getting higher now, like she could obviously tell that I was trying to keep something from her. And I was, but for how long could I manage that? She'd get it out of me eventually.

"Jay Sinclair, for the love of all that's holy! Tell me where my Brinky's gone!"

I told her and then held my breath, the same way that you might do when a pistol fires and you're left waiting to find out who the bullet hits. But her response was not like any mere gunshot. It was far more like a volley of artillery.

"He *what?* With *who?* That *lunatic?* That evil *slut?* How could you let this *happen*, Jay?"

"I'm not his father, last time that I looked," I stuttered.

"Brinky's such an innocent! So gentle and so sweet! And so easily taken advantage of! You should have been looking *after* him!"

"But Midge—I hate to say this—isn't that your job?"

All I got by way of a response was the disconnect tone ringing in my ears, so she had hung up violently. I wasn't all that fond of Midge but still felt bad, since she was clearly horribly upset.

The next evening, sometime around nine, I was just pouring out the final drops of Chateau Cartier when I heard hooves on the road outside, accompanied by a low rumble of wheels, and those sounds stopped directly outside my place. Heels vibrated on my porch. There came a sturdy rap on my front door.

Midge—her proper name was Millicent—stood there in the gathering gloom, her attention going venomously to the glass in my left hand before returning to my face.

She had on a pale blue dress, a fringe at the bottom, and a fashionable cloche hat, the first showing off her rather pudgy figure and the latter emphasizing her round face. But her eyes—a tepid shade of brown—were as hard as steel and seemed to almost burn.

The carriage behind her was the same cab which had brought me here, with the same driver at the reins—she'd obviously instructed him to wait. And propped up next to the passenger seat was a huge metal steamer trunk, so Midge had obviously done a lot of packing before coming here.

She was glowering at me as though I personally might be responsible for all the trouble in the world.

"What kind of place is this?" she snapped. "There are no police here, none at all. Did you know that?"

"You tried to contact them?"

"I also tried to phone the mad slut's house. She either doesn't have a telephone or has no listed number."

"And so ... what is it that you want me to do about it, Midge?"

"Are you friendly with this Gorsting woman?"

"I wouldn't say so. Why d'you ask?"

"I tried to get in there but the gate is locked. And so I stood there like a perfect idiot, yelling out at the top of my voice. I must have shouted out for almost twenty minutes, except not a single curtain moved and no one tried to answer me."

Which seemed like an odd way to act, even for the Gorsting place. When I'd gone there the first time they had let me in quite easily. And I could see why Midge had cause to be concerned, but wasn't sure how I could help.

"I was hoping you might know a way in there."

"I'm really sorry, Midge, but no, I don't. But why discuss this on the porch? Would you like to come inside?"

"I'm not here for your hospitality. I'm here to get my Brinky back, and if you are of no use in that I'll gladly take my leave of you."

"And then go and do what?" I asked her in a puzzled tone.

And in a quite concerned way too. As I've already pointed out, Midge—like her fiancé—wasn't very smart or practical.

"I'm going to sit outside that house until they are forced to acknowledge me. I'll stay there the whole night if need be. They can't ignore me forever."

I already knew what Anastasia was like, though. She played to no one else's rules, and definitely wouldn't let her hand be forced. And so Midge here might find herself sitting there for several days. I tried to keep my voice as reasonable as I could.

"If I'm going to be honest, then that really doesn't sound like too much of a plan. Why don't you stop here tonight, and we can do something about it in the morning's light."

Her only response was a stiff shake of her head and she stared at me with quite open contempt.

"I've never really liked you, Jay. You're far too smooth for your own good. And now you've gone and smoothed my precious Brinky into trouble of some kind. But you'll do that no more. Please stay away from us."

She was blaming me for all of this, in other words. And having made that very plain, she turned smartly on her heels and headed back in the direction of the cab. The driver wheeled his vehicle around and then they trotted back off toward the poetess's residence.

I was forced to watch as that bend in the lane went and swallowed up another person that I knew. The big dark house beyond it seemed to be some kind of terminus, a hole into which people disappeared and sometimes did not reemerge.

The hell with Midge, though, with her rude abrasive stares and tart retorts! If she sat there till she passed out, what business of it was mine? She had really annoyed me and my thoughts were clouded, so I slammed the door shut and then did my best to put her right out of my mind. I downed the rest of the Bordeaux and then lit a new cigar, and with that clamped between my teeth I plumped myself down on my couch and resumed my reading of the Sinclair Lewis book.

I was almost at the final chapter, but was having trouble making my eyes follow it. And I was chewing on the cigar so fiercely that its end was breaking up.

I've never really liked you, Jay. Well that was mutual, wasn't it? But my conscience had started troubling me, and vague dim images kept on flashing through my head of something quite unpleasant happening to her. What kind of 'unpleasant' I was not entirely sure, but she was on her own out there, and it was simply not in my nature to leave any woman in that state of vulnerability.

Night had closed fully around the house, one of those bottomless Sauquill nights with not a sound emerging from the darkness. And had Midge been expecting anything like that? I doubted it. And was she getting scared? Cursing underneath my breath, I put the novel to one side and went back out.

There were still no other noises here save for the faint murmur of a constant breeze. Cloud was swirling overhead, so that no stars could be made out and I could only catch some fractured glimpses of the moon. Maybe I should go and find a flashlight, but I'd traveled this lane many times, so I set off on foot. The further from my place I got though, then the more I felt my unease grow.

My footsteps seemed impossibly loud, crunching on the shallow gravel. I was even aware of my own breathing and it was a harsh, stentorian sound. I was going around the wide arc in the road by now. And halfway along it, the clouds covered up the moon completely, so that my surroundings went entirely black. I tried to take another step but wobbled and pulled back again. I felt like I was standing on a cliff, quite uncertain where the edge might be.

Your lighter, idiot! I pulled it out and flicked it on. Which was not enough to truly reveal anything, but at least it gave me some sense of perspective. I was able to head on again.

My surroundings were mostly a blank, a hollow not unlike the opening to a cave. And my imagination started running wild. Might there be something else out here with me? I slowed down and listened, and the only sound that I could hear at first was thin twigs humming as they caught the breeze.

But then, in the tall grasses to my right, there came a brief and swift rustle that I could not put down to the wind. I couldn't even see those grasses but felt absolutely certain they had just been moved. And then, to my left, a tree branch creaked, like something heavy might be pressing down on it. So I went forward as quickly as I dared. And the noises, thank the heavens, didn't follow me.

A few lights from the Gorsting home finally swung into view, but it was not electric lighting I was looking at. She did have that—I knew it from the last time I'd been here. But now it had been switched off and been replaced at several windows by a very different kind of glow, a flickering sort of sheen that had a waxy yellow hue. This was either lamps or candles I was looking at, and why should the mistress of this hideous abode have resorted to such as that?

Perhaps it was a part of the dark Romanticism which clearly governed her wild fractured soul, a need for mysticism and a love of the arcane. Or perhaps she had a suitor in her house tonight. There was simply no way to know.

My gaze went across to the tall iron fence, hoping to make out the dim outline of Miss Midge Ellmans sitting on her steamer trunk. But she wasn't there.

Every other matter was forgotten in a flash. My heartbeat quickened and my mouth felt dry. I walked across and tried to scan the lane as far as the deep gloom would let me, but I couldn't catch the tiniest glimpse of Brinkley Breslaw's fiancée. I found some wheel-tracks from the cab she'd used, but they continued past this property apparently without a pause.

And Midge had been so firmly settled on that stupid shallow-witted plan of hers, utterly convinced that if she stuck it out then she would get her Brinky back. So where exactly had she gone ... had they actually relented and then let her in? I went over to the gate and rattled it, but it proved to be firmly locked.

Puzzlement enfolded me, except that I could not imagine what it was I should do next. Save for the soft pulsing of that yellow glow, the house was absolutely still, so this business wasn't going to be resolved tonight. Perhaps the morning would cast fresher light on it.

I found myself with no choice but to head back wearily the way I'd come. And just before I caught sight of my home again, I genuinely *did* hear another noise.

It was a pair of very large wings, flapping softly overhead.

iii

I only slept shallowly that night, and woke up the next morning with a startled jerk. My alarm clock told me it was just past dawn, so Midge's disappearance was still bothering me, even while I was asleep. And that being the case, I did not allow myself my usual languorous morning-time routine, but simply dragged some clothes on, swilled my mouth out and then headed for my bike.

Sauquill Island seemed quieter than ever as I sped along, the colorless light of a cloudy dawn giving it the chilled appearance of some frozen tundra to the north. The breeze had stopped, the trees were still and no shapes moved across the sky. I stopped again outside the Gorsting residence and found the front gate was still locked. I would return here later if I must, but I pressed on to Marinsberg.

The walls and low roofs of the little town welled up in my vision before too much longer. Except that here was something I had never seen when I had visited before. Whenever I had come here previously, there had been almost nobody about, the cobbled streets empty and the stores devoid of customers.

Only that right now I could make out movement. Not too much of it, but there were definitely people out of doors. From this distance, they appeared as little more than low hunched shapes whose details I could not make out. Men or women, young or old? It was impossible to tell, and so I pushed my pedals harder, trying to get close. Several heads came up, however, at the sound of my approach. Panic seemed to grip them, spur them into action, and they quickly drifted out of sight, into smaller alleys or else back inside their homes.

The result being that the town was quite deserted again by the time my wheels were bumping down its avenues. Why had its inhabitants retreated that way, and why were they abroad at only this ungodly hour? More bemused than ever, I continued on toward the quay.

And was relieved to see a familiar figure there. The same cabbie was standing by the dock, watering his shabby horse. He too looked up when he heard me coming and he favored me with a perfunctory nod, but otherwise he did not move.

His face looked much slacker than it had been the first time I'd encountered him. His eyes, which were a murky green, seemed to be focused on some unknown distance and were noticeably lifeless and dim. But I contrived to ignore all that.

"Hey there!" I greeted him, climbing from my saddle.

His horse snorted nervously and clacked its hooves, but its owner simply peered at me from underneath his Derby hat.

"I've never caught your name," I tried, in an attempt to break the ice.

There was a thoughtful pause, then "Saul," came the reply. His voice had lost all of the jollity and humor that had been there earlier on, but I did my best to ignore that as well.

"Jay," I came back at him. "But tell me, Saul, that passenger you had last night, that rather bossy young woman? She led me to believe that she would have you set her down outside the Gorsting house, except that doesn't actually seem to be the case."

"Changed her mind, she did," he said, and he twitched his shoulders gently.

"Is that right?"

"Ordered me to bring her right back here, where she was just in time to catch the ferry to the mainland."

"I had no idea the service ran that late."

"The motor on that lousy boat is always breaking down, and so it set off back for Providence much later than it ought have done. A stroke of luck for the lady with her trunk, since she'd have had to wait the whole night otherwise."

Midge changing her mind so fast? A passenger craft which broke down constantly? None of this sounded fully right to me.

"That runt the captain has on board," the cabbie was still going on, "Bobsnitch, I believe he's called—he doesn't look like much and isn't very bright, but he seems to have a talent when it comes to fixing stuff."

But was Saul doing no more than embellishing a set of lies? I gazed across at Narragansett Sound, wondering where the ferry was right now. Perhaps the captain could confirm this tale? But there were no vessels in sight ... it was too early in the day for that.

So I left Saul behind and started back. And during that entire trip, the same suspicion kept on worrying at me as had done after I had heard that scream. That the explanations I'd received were carefully and meticulously rehearsed and fell short of the actual truth.

It was no more than an impression, though, and I had no way of proving that.

The gate was still locked when I regained the Gorsting house, and still with not a sign of movement beyond it.

iv

Two nights later on, there was another of those wretched parties. Carriages and bicycle wheels rolling past my porch again. A babbling of voices that rose louder and became so fierce at times it was hard to believe that it was civilized people making such sounds. The blue-green light came on again, but this time rising in a column so high it pressed against the moving clouds and painted them its diseased hue. And the poetess was on her balcony again, calling out so stridently that I could hear her every word.

"That is not dead which can eternal lie! And with strange eons even death may die!"

An excerpt from another of her poems, doubtless, and the unseen mob below whooped its approval.

She headed off the balcony again, and must have gone down to circulate, because the babbling of her guests grew more frenzied and took on almost a delirious tone.

But then it stopped. Not died away but ceased between one second and the next. Utter silence hung across the landscape for a while.

And then that sheer and total hush was broken by a warbling cry. A woman's voice, and rising higher until it reached a falsetto peak. Then it simply stopped as well, broke off abruptly and it came no more.

It wasn't possible another guest had had a fit, if that had even been the reality. I clenched my fists and found my palms were wet. What the blazes were they doing over there?

v

It was pretty much impossible to identify who'd screamed, and I was aware of that. It had been a woman I had heard for sure, but raised high in terror or in pain, any voice takes on a shapeless quality. Renewed suspicions were nagging at me though, and so I hunted through my address book until I found the number for the Ellmans residence in the Back Bay.

And was pleased to hear a familiar voice when someone finally picked up. I'm not friendly with too many older skirts, but Esmeralda Ellmans— Midge's mother—was a genuine exception to that rule. A doyenne of Boston's upper ranks ever since I'd been a little kid, she had a fine sharp wit, a lively tongue, and such a predilection for good common sense that, were there any proper justice in this world, she would be sitting on the Supreme Court. How she'd spawned a dunce like Millicent was anybody's guess, but maybe I could finally make some sense of this.

"Jackson? But how are you, boy? I've been told that you're not round here anymore, and I was sad to hear it. Why is that?"

I took a minute filling her in, than posed the question I was dying to ask.

"Is Millicent at home?"

"No, I'm afraid she's not."

And Esmeralda's voice became a little duller as she spoke those words. I reminded myself that she was fairly elderly and that I was phoning her quite late.

"The reason being?"

"She's gotten on a plane and flown away to Paris."

What? She'd gone off to join up with the Lost Generation? I tried to imagine dumb Midge Ellmans conversing with Hemingway or Ezra Pound and I could not. Was this some kind of joke?

"You're *sure* of that, Esme?"

"Why wouldn't I be?"

"And is Brinkley with her?"

"I believe he's not."

Esmeralda's entire tone, by now, had taken on a soporific quality, as though she might be falling half-asleep while still in the act of talking to me. And I'd never known her to behave like that.

"I believe they had some kind of row," she was mumbling. "You know how volatile young people are."

Except that Midge had not *seen* Brink when she had visited this place, and I told her mother that. She turned that information over with a slowness that was not her style.

"Maybe it was not a row, then. Maybe she was simply angry at the company that he was keeping. That infernal poetess? Who knows what could be going on behind closed doors? But she was furious with him, I'm sure of that. And so she's gone to Paris on her own."

"She *told* you all of that?"

"She …" And Esmeralda paused again, like she was trying to delve back through her failing, foggy memories. "I think she phoned from Providence. Yes, I'm sure that was the case. I recall her saying …"

But then the woman's voice, it trailed off altogether.

"Esme?" I tried.

All I got back was a clatter as she put the handset down. And when I tried to phone again, I could only hear the engaged tone and that deeply puzzled me.

Except I had no way of knowing at the time how powerful the influence of Cthulhu was, how far it reached and how profoundly it could infect somebody's mind and fill it up with blatant lies.

CHAPTER TEN

PROVIDENCE AND BACK

i

The next few weeks dragged past in a fairly leaden way, the weather often poor, my progress with *The Belles of Boston* faltering and uncertain, my evenings only ever enlivened by the playing of my jazz collection. Not that the quietness of my existence bothered me too much—I had grown accustomed to it—except that one matter genuinely bothered me. Over the course of this month, I had put the invitation out to a lot of friends to come and visit me at my new island residence but, Brink Breslaw apart, not one of them had accepted it. Nobody came knocking at my door, and my telephone did not ring again.

I've never really liked you, Jay. You're far too smooth for your own good. Was that how other people genuinely saw me, so they did not care that I was gone? It sometimes kept me up at night.

Toward the end of that month, I got some information from Mr. Arnold Sewell—when I went by for a fresh batch of cigars—that genuinely surprised me and alarmed me slightly too. I had always taken the ferry service here for granted, only it turned out that, from September onward, it got cut down to just several times a week, and much less than that the following month, and only when the severity of the sea allowed.

I had been here on Sauquill for a good long while now, and the knowledge that I might be trapped here raised in me an almost feverish urge to visit the mainland one more time, so to reacquaint myself with normal life and with the vibrant business of a proper city. And it was in that way that I was waiting on the dock at nine o'clock the next Tuesday morning when the ferry boat showed up.

The same captain was at the wheel, still chewing on a portion of a dead cheroot. And that deformed homunculus—Bobsnitch, was it?—came leaping out and fastened the mooring ropes, then jumped back in and curled into a ball again.

A couple of passengers got off, but I turned out to be the only person heading back. I paid my fare and climbed aboard and, seeing as how there was only me, the boat swung round and headed back out to sea.

The engine chugged, a pleasant rhythmic sound. And I know that this is odd, but you can always smell the sea considerably more strongly once that you are out on it, rather than just standing by the shore. Salty ozone filled my nostrils and revived my spirits and my general mood.

We were perhaps three hundred yards out by this stage. Staring back, I studied the vista I'd been living in—the small gray town, still and lifeless; the utter and uncompromising flatness of the landscape out beyond; and off to the right-hand side, the mysterious Plinth, still glittering faintly in the weak daylight.

But then we cleared the swathe of cloud that had been hanging over Sauquill and were plunged into a proper August day, bright hot sunlight beating down. There was still a breeze but even that was warm. I took off my jacket and I tipped my face toward the sun, receiving its rays gratefully.

Then something else occurred to me; a question that I had to ask. I got up from my seat and walked across and sat down on a gunwale right next to the captain, who favored me with an uncertain glance.

"You had another passenger a few weeks back? A round-faced woman with a steamer trunk?"

"Well, yes, I remember her. She insisted me and Bobsnitch carry the damned thing aboard, and it felt to me like it was filled with cannonballs."

"She came and left on the same day, returning to the mainland after night had fallen?"

The skipper fell silent for longer than seemed natural, his gaze becoming rather faded. But then he recovered and gave a sharp nod.

"She did. That's true."

It had been a while since Midge had been here, so perhaps that memory had gotten slightly lost. But now the matter seemed to be resolved. Wherever Midge Ellmans might be, she definitely wasn't here.

We continued chugging steadily toward the coast, Narragansett Bay in clear and open view now, small cities like Newport apparent on the islands that we'd have to skirt around in order to reach Providence. And I was beginning to enjoy this trip when the engine gave a noisy sputter and cut out.

The captain cursed, although not violently, which made it very plain that this was—as the cabbie Saul had pointed out—far from an unusual circumstance.

"Bobsnitch?" came the shout. And the captain pointed to the stern.

His crewman warily uncurled himself, his big protruding eyes blinking, his dirty-looking skin—and I could see this time that there were whole great swathes of scabs on it—revealing its unnatural color to the clear daylight. Raising himself up, as much as he could with a back as bent as that, he threw me a suspicious glance then went around the ferry's other side to attend to the motor. He had very long thin fingers, I took note, and kept on letting out curious low grunting murmurs as he went about his work.

But we were out now on the open sea without any form of propulsion, the ship no longer on a forward course but drifting sideways at the mercy of the tides. And the deck had taken on a sickening slant, a violent swaying that had not been there previously. I immediately became concerned, since our prospects seemed uncertain by this point. Might a large wave swamp us, so we'd come to harm?

And I was still in the grip of anxiety of that sort when, without any least fanfare, the sea began to calm right down, its surface nearly flattening out. And I figured that this had to be the same curious phenomenon I had witnessed from the shore, as if there was some sort of large obstruction underneath the boat.

I leant across the side and peered into the ocean's depths. And I could see nothing but swirling limpid green at first, the sunlight penetrating deep. But still I got the distinct impression that there was something right down there below us, large enough to calm the waves and stave the tidal currents off. I could not see the thing but I could *feel* it, which makes no sense and I get that. But a dire kind of foreboding had begun to close around me now, a fear of something that refused to show itself, a fear indeed of the Unknown. A freezing chill had hardened in my gut and all of my sinews had tightened up. There was something down there in the depths and I was absolutely certain of it.

But then the engine gave a brisk rattle and chugged back into life again. Bobsnitch went immediately to the prow and resumed his hunkered down position. And the ferry swung back northward and continued on its normal course, and I found myself being drawn out of the fearful reverie that I had fallen into, and came to see it had been little more than that. Being adrift and rendered helpless ... it had made me very nervous, yes. And in that state of fraught anxiety, my imagination had been playing tricks on me.

I put those kinds of worries behind me the best way that I could, and we continued without any further incident to the fair city of Providence itself.

ii

The quays were bustling once again, Chinese and Hispanics, Africans and even Lascars hard at work in each direction that I looked, the sun still hot and our surroundings clear. But mostly I felt rather parched, the salty journey and that unscheduled delay and the heat of the daylight drying up my mouth and throat. And so I kept on heading down until I found an open-air cafe, parasols spread over the ornate metal tables.

The only trouble was that they were mostly full, and largely with big noisy families. This was August after all, and so most of these folks had to be day-trippers, enjoying the weather and the fresh sea breeze.

A table at the far end, though, was only being occupied by one lone man, a decidedly narrow fellow several years younger than me, with large ears and a compact mouth and with eyes that boggled very slightly underneath his wide flat brow. There was a cup of coffee placed in front of him and a copy of the *Boston Globe* folded tightly beside that, but he was ignoring them both and scribbling in a large notebook.

I stopped beside him.

"Do you mind?"

In response, he gave a start and looked up at me anxiously, and so it looked to be the case that this was a rather nervous kind of fellow.

"If I take one of these other seats?" I tried again. "Is that okay?"

He nodded and then turned his face away from me, returning his attention to his notes. A waitress showed up and I ordered an iced tea. But sheer politeness forbade me from leaving this encounter just at that.

"I'm Jackson," I told my new companion, "but most people call me Jay."

"Howard," he replied, not even glancing up, "and people never call me anything but that."

And beyond that point he contrived to behave as though I was not even there. My drink showed up; I sipped it gratefully and watched the people all around me, but my focus was gradually drawn back to the folded-up newspaper on our tabletop.

"Okay if I take a look? I haven't seen one of these in quite a while."

Howard nodded unconcernedly, with his head still down.

I opened up the *Globe* and saw the banner headline read: COOLIDGE RESUMES TALKS ON THE GERMAN ECONOMY.

Which—I found out from the first couple of paragraphs—had collapsed altogether like a stack of pebbles in the middle of this month. Cut off from the regular world as I had been, I'd had no way of knowing of that event. But … why on earth should the VP be heading up discussions such as these? I put that question to this Howard too, and the response I got was quite dramatic.

He immediately forgot about his notes. His face came up and stayed there and he stared at me with open shock.

"Warren Harding died quite suddenly three weeks ago and Calvin Coolidge was sworn in. Where have you been living, man, in a cavern at the bottom of the sea?"

I tried to get my head around that piece of news and imagine how it must have been. All the flags around me would have been flown at half-mast. Both the funeral and the inauguration would have been broadcast on the radio. And I'd been deaf and blind to all of that, which proved to me—in devastating terms—how isolated I'd become. Almost flushing with embarrassment, I explained to the man where I had been.

And when I mentioned Sauquill Island, Howard's manner took a sharp turn for the worse. His face went even paler and he stared wide-eyed in the direction of that place, although you could not even see it from this vantage point.

"I have lived in these environs all my life," he explained in a low hushed voice, "and many times I have stood upon its coast as twilight falls and gazed across the water at the place of which you speak. And every time I have done that, I have felt a horrible anxiety envelop me. That island has a loathsome aspect, a dark miasma hanging over it which is unnatural and entirely foul, and I suspect that there are Nameless Forces at work on its shores."

Which little speech convinced me of one thing … that this fellow I'd sat down beside was some kind of oddball of the highest order. Who knew what insane and rambling fantasies he might be scribbling in his book? I quickly finished up my drink, bade him a good day, then walked off into the city's streets.

And I spent a couple of hours exploring them quite cheerfully, the tall pale buildings and the cleanly-swept thoroughfares. Cars and taxicabs were humming by and the sidewalks were full of busy people. In the relaxed frame of mind that I was in, I even nodded and smiled at a couple of them as I passed, except they did not seem to notice or acknowledge me. I thought that pretty odd at first, but perhaps it was the case that the inhabitants here were not nearly as open as my native Boston's residents.

I finally came across a French-style bistro where I settled down for lunch, and was forced to acknowledge what a real pleasure it was to eat a meal which had been prepared by someone who knew how to cook.

Stepping out again, and following my nose, I happened across a movie theatre—no great big deal in itself. Except a small white poster that was slapped across a larger one had just three words printed upon it. *Now With Sound.*

I'd never heard of such a thing. But it had to be, apparently, another miracle of this new age. And so I paid for a ticket and I went on in, and sat there in the darkness utterly transfixed as three short films were projected on the screen in which the actors seemed to actually talk to me. It was an experience that filled me up with awe, like seeing massive gray-edged ghosts emerging from the spirit world and being brought back properly to life. I was still in the grip of wonder when I finally stumbled out.

And in an invigorated and positive frame of mind, I made my way to Roger Williams Park, where I strolled through the pleasant greenery and tried to let it calm me down. There were vibrant flowers in the Japanese and Rose gardens and noises from the caged beasts in the nearby zoo, and families were camped out on the grass, but there were lots of younger adults too. Students from Brown and from Rhode Island College by the blazers some of them were wearing; healthy, hearty boys and slender pretty girls as well, and my attention went particularly to those.

What did I think that I was even *doing*, stuck out where I was these days? I had become a virtual recluse, my waking hours bled of color and true incident and of lively company. Maybe I should just throw in the whole kit and caboodle, jump on board the next train back and forget about the island and the rented house.

Except that felt like giving up, and that was not like me in the least bit. I'd come out here to make a real name for myself, one that went beyond my family's wealth. And sure, the novel wasn't going all that well, but nobody had ever claimed that writing was an easy job. I should at least go back and fetch my manuscript before I moved away.

But first things first. I was watching the girls again, and beginning to feel an itch I sorely needed half a chance to scratch. There was a rank of cabs beside the entrance to the zoo, their uniformed drivers lolling idly about. And, making some discreet enquiries and passing a few singles round, I found out the location of a secret kind of meeting place—it proved to be only two blocks from here.

I reached the appropriate door, knocked four times on it as I had been told, and a slot came open at face-height, a flinty pair of eyes appraising me. After that, there was a walk down a short corridor till I came to a second door, and when that opened ragtime music, cigarette smoke and the distinctive smell of liquor all washed over me.

iii

Even in the capital of such a tiny state, you could still find a speakeasy. The place was packed and the illumination dim, red shades round the light fittings. But for myself, I felt at home at last. These kinds of people were my own.

I didn't focus too much on the men. The women, who outnumbered them, looked as if they'd all been cut from very similar molds indeed, with bobbed hairstyles and fringed short skirts, darkly-painted lips and eyes that seemed to almost strain under the sheer weight of the mascara on their lashes. This—since Prohibition had come in—had been my favorite kind of haunt. And I took to it eagerly, since illegality brings out the wild side in most women.

"Hi, there. I'm Jackson of the Sinclair clan ... you might have heard of us? But most people call me –"

A willowy brunette with a stunning heart-shaped face glanced up at me with interest at first, but then her eyes lost all their focus and she swiveled off.

"Hello. You can call me Jay. And I should call you?"

A slim waif with her blonde hair done in curly ringlets opened her mouth to reply, but then she seemed to change her mind. Her lips snapped shut and she actually frowned, then turned her back on me and moved off through the crowd.

What, did I have something stuck between my teeth? I checked on that and felt sure I did not. And so I pushed my way through to the counter, trying to catch the bartenders' attention, but they didn't seem to notice me.

Lively talk was echoing through the room like thunder rolling on some distant hill, but none of it was directed at me. Nobody seemed conscious I was here. I'd found myself, by this stage of the game, surrounded by a wall of raised shoulders and backs. Someone to the left of me was describing a Red Sox game, and I did my best to break into that conversation, but it was like they couldn't hear my voice.

What the *hell* was happening now? At over six foot tall and reasonably well-built, I'd never had the slightest trouble getting other people to engage with me. I finally managed to get a drink and knocked it back in one swift gulp ... that made me screw my eyelids briefly shut, and I thought that I could make out something writhing in the darkness there. More visions of tentacles, perhaps? And why did I keep seeing those?

But I was heading out of that establishment in less than half an hour, my elevated mood of earlier gone, my optimism torn to shreds and a deep feeling of gloom settling down around me. Had those people back in the speakeasy sensed that I no longer belonged? That I had turned myself into a hermit, all my charm and social graces lost?

Except that I now understand the truth of this. In his sunken city, far beneath the ocean waves, Lord Cthulhu sleeps. But it is not a flat and shapeless slumber such as gathers up us human beings—it has focus and intent, is telepathic, and it reaches out and touches people's minds and bends them to his will.

Cthulhu did not *want* me to be happy on the mainland. Did not *want* me to leave Sauquill Island. No, he had a purpose for me.

I was bait.

iv

I wandered slowly, awkwardly, throughout the city's streets another while, attempting to recapture the positive mood that had gripped me earlier on, but it had vanished like the morning mist. The crowds had thinned out on the streets and clouds had moved in overhead, maybe following me across from Sauquill, or at least it felt that way.

I *still* couldn't figure out why I'd been snubbed in such a fashion, and continued brooding on it as I headed back toward the docks.

It was a wait of well over an hour before the ferry boat showed up again. The light had started falling as I climbed aboard. Once again, I was the only passenger.

"Is the motor okay now?"

The captain only pursed his lips, then set us off toward the open water.

There were other islands visible when we got there; New Shoreham to the west, the Vineyard to the east, and I thought that I could even see the vaguest outline of Nantucket out past that. But it was Sauquill itself that held my attention the most. The clouds above it were still dense and gave the light descending on the place an oddly dismal, brooding quality.

A 'dark miasma,' as that guy at the café had said. And, quite peculiar though he had been, perhaps he had a solid point.

The daylight was diminishing at an even faster rate, the sun sinking down off to the west in a display of bronze and coppery red that washed across the ocean's surface, tinting it a sanguine color. And, as often happens at this time of the day, the breeze dropped away and our surroundings became calmer.

A good long way off to my left-hand side, what looked to be a dense black head came popping up, just as I'd seen happen off the beach where I had found that parasol. It was too far distant to make features out, but I felt sure that the eyes in it had to be regarding us. It remained there for just a couple of seconds before ducking back beneath the brine. But then there were a couple of swirls and I believed I caught a fleeting glimpse of a dark back. I pointed these facts out to the captain.

"My guess would be they are some breed of seal," he told me. "Always been here, they have, but they're awful shy. They never ever come too close, and if you try to approach them they disappear in one swift flash."

I couldn't help but notice, though, that the homunculus Bobsnitch had uncurled a touch—his face was poking out from underneath one arm and he was sniffing at the evening air as though he had detected something.

Marinsberg was coming fully into view. Cloaked in twilight as it was, it looked grayer than it ever had, a crouching place, a huddled place, as dormant as a drunken hobo asleep in some shabby doorway. There were almost no lights on at all, despite the fact that it was almost fully night.

But then I caught a glimpse of movement in the little square just past the quay. Shapes were on the move out there, dim figures shifting slowly round.

Finally and at long last, the place was showing signs of proper life. I peered hard but could not see these people clearly, since there was no lamplight and the moon was covered up.

Bobsnitch seemed to recognize them though, because he was already on his feet, the mooring rope in one thin hand. As we drew closer to the dock, he jumped much earlier than he usually did, his legs flailing eagerly. He barely made it to the edge of the jetty, but that didn't seem to bother him. The rope was fastened to a bollard in an instant and then he was heading off.

He joined the others that I'd seen. They seemed to be familiar, since several of them grasped him by the shoulders. And then the entire group—and there were maybe eight or ten of them—went scampering off into the gloom, the dimness of the evening swallowing them up. But just before they disappeared, I thought that I could make some particulars out.

Such as bent backs and swollen foreheads. Bulging eyes and upper limbs that were too long and lower ones that bent off to the sides and gave their owners an inhuman waddle.

They were gone altogether before too much longer, but I felt astonished all the same. I had always assumed that Bobsnitch was merely a lone unfortunate, some singular freak, a miscarriage of Nature. But it was now proven that was not the truth. No, there were others like him in this place, the same as him, and so not to be explained as an accident of birth.

More as though their genesis was planned. Like some of the women round here had been interbreeding with another biped species.

But there *were* no others that I knew of, not around these parts. So … what?

CHAPTER ELEVEN

THE PERIL FROM THE OCEAN

i

The attack on my house came in mid-September.

My days had fused into a seamless blur by then, a constant round of sleeping, attempting to write some more, eating a sparse meal then dozing in my living room. I was not even playing my records anymore.

The bottles of Bushmills kept arriving on my porch and I received them gratefully, since they were my sole diversion now. I do not think I even noticed the increasingly strong effect that they were having on my consciousness. I was sleeping far longer than was usually my habit, and when I was not trying to work—or sometimes even when I was—my thoughts would slip off into idle, pointless wanderings. Was the whisky being drugged? That might be possible, perhaps.

But the weather kept on getting worse as well, totally unseasonable for this time of the year.

Early on a Wednesday evening, a storm started blowing up. The sky, which was already gray, went several shades darker in a bare few minutes and the wind changed direction sharply, coming in from the north-east and moaning round my rafters like some hungry hunting animal. Rain was slapping on my window panes, and as the dimness deepened to sheer black the fury of the climate increased fast.

A gale was screeching viciously by nine o'clock. Gazing out through a back window, I could see some lights on in the Gorsting home, and silhouetted against those the trees between her residence and mine were being bent over almost double. I began to worry that my own roof might come off.

My doors and windows were all rattling, so I went quickly round the house checking that they were secure, pressing latches firmly into place and turning the keys in the locks both front and back. Thank God that I did that, or I would not be here.

I had just secured the front door of the place, and had moved to the window beside it. There was the faintest hint of moonlight out, the clouds having been pushed into long narrow strips by the ferocious force of this wild storm. And I was alarmed to realize I could see the ocean's waves clearly from all the way back here, something that had never been the case before. Massive ones were striking up against the shore with such brute force and energy that they were sending huge plumes up into the air, rising twenty feet or more.

Then something else began moving off in that direction, something in the grassy stretch between my homestead and the coast. And whatever it might be, it was fully-defined and dark and large. An animal, was my first thought, the first of such things I had seen—the dismal scared horses apart—since I had moved into this place. I tried my best to fathom what it was, but in the dimness and the howling murk I couldn't be entirely sure.

There was only one light switched on in my living room; its glow was reflecting on the inside of the window pane and hampering my view. And so I went across and switched it off, then went back for a clearer look. And I got nothing at first, since the moon had disappeared again. But when a section of it reemerged, the scene that it revealed made me freeze up.

There was not simply one unknown figure on the move out there. No, but there were three and they were standing upright. Hulking shapes that seemed to be completely black, and coming forward with a curious kind of motion, a hopping, flapping, flopping kind of gait, as though their legs were partly fused together and they were incapable of walking in a normal way.

These were men though, no doubt about that, and big ones too with broad shoulders and thickened limbs. And they were moving steadily toward my place. I could not figure out where precisely they had come from … there were no houses or even roads off in that direction. And they could not have arrived here on any vessel. The seas around this isle had become far too rough.

But they kept on coming till they'd almost reached the lane, and I was in no doubt where they were headed to.

I had never felt so isolated as I did in that one moment of stark realization, the whole world shrinking down to the size of my living room and everything beyond it gone. And was the room shaking now, or was it only me? Every single move I made was stiff and slow and seemed to take forever. But I backed off from the window and began to try and think what weapons I could count upon if they were needed to defend myself. I owned no guns … I'd never had the slightest use for those things. And yes, this room had a fireplace, but it had never been lit up and there were no irons in it. There were knives back in the kitchen though, and I stumbled through and selected the largest one. But when I returned to the living room and stared out through the window again, I could make out not a hint of those three hulking crippled men.

Something clattered on the wooden boards of my front porch. A heavy sound, so something out of sight but large was on the move out there. I lifted the knife to shoulder height, its handle greasy in my grasp.

My doorknob gave a swift, sharp rattle. Someone had just tested it and, finding it to be locked, paused an instant and then thumped against the woodwork in frustration. The door held firm but I jerked back, and I was shivering now and fighting for every breath.

Noises from the kitchen told me that the same was happening round the back. All three figures were apparently at the walls of the house by now—I was surrounded in the raging dark. The wind kept howling and the rain kept coming down, and all that made my situation worse, because I could not properly tell what was going on outside.

A shadow appeared for just the briefest moment at my window pane. And it was moving in the same strange way, but this close up it looked considerably less human. Its head was too large and of oddest shape, bulging hugely at the brow and with a jaw so large and heavy it was almost hanging loosely from its hinges. And its shoulders seemed to have an oily gleam to them, reflecting the dim sheen of moonlight in the same way fish scales might.

That was the impression I received, except the shape was there and gone within a taut blink of my startled eyes.

There was an abrupt sliding, rasping noise from over to my left-hand side. I swung toward it, but there was only a wall off there. So I could only try and guess what I was listening to, and it took me ages to arrive at a conclusion. One of those figures out there—though by what means I could not tell—was slowly climbing up the outside of this place. The sound went on for practically a minute and then stopped, so had the climber given up?

There was a sudden sharp report from practically above my head, a whole big glass pane being smashed. A window up there had been broken through, which meant that one of these intruders was by now inside the house. Enfolded in the darkness, feeling smothered by it, I crouched down and waited to find out what was going to happen next.

A floorboard creaked above me. Was this invader moving to the stairs? I wanted to get out of here, simply abandon my home and run, but I was not sure that that was at all wise. If I went bursting out through the front door, I might well find myself going directly into the fierce clutches of the other two. Better to stay put, I tried to tell myself, or for the while at least. So, squatting down like some small frightened child, I clutched the knife handle in both my hands and tried unsuccessfully to keep my breathing quiet.

The floorboards above me were still groaning—the intruder was on the upper landing now. My mind was working feverishly but not settling upon any course of action that made realistic sense. Stay put or flee? Fight or submit? I could not decide which was best, since I had no idea exactly what my situation was.

When suddenly, from the direction of the lane, a voice rang out imperiously. A female voice, and one I recognized, although I could not understand a single thing that she was saying.

"S'shagh ger'quast!" I thought I heard.

The screeching wind was ripping at each syllable so very fiercely that it wasn't clear.

"Gnak ud wahwe!"

And what kind of tongue was that? Except the creaking of the boards above my head had stopped, and nobody was putting any further weight on my front and back doors.

Another few phrases of apparent gibberish were shouted out, only it was the final word that properly caught my attention. I had heard it before, although I'd thought it to be 'Zulu' at the time.

That was not right, and I could tell that now. It was, in fact, a lot more like *Kuh-thoo-loo.*

But its effect was electric. The next sound that reached my ears, another rattling on my porch, was one of these attackers moving off it. And I could make out hurried flopping down the house's side, presumably the fellow who had gone to my back door. As for the invader in the rooms above, he was heading for the window and he must have jumped, because I heard a heavy thumping on the ground below.

Rigid and still shivering, I managed to unbend my knees and stood up sufficiently that I could see out through my front window again. A bolt of lightning flashed across the sky, revealing all three burly figures heading back the way they'd come.

I dropped the knife at that point, wiped slick perspiration from my face and then let out a long harsh breath. My heart was pounding like I'd run ten miles, but everything else was numb.

I waited until my head had stopped whirling and then switched the light back on. And then I went to my front door, fumbling at the latch with stiff, unfeeling hands.

Anastasia Gorsting was standing right there on my porch.

ii

She was barely wet at all, and the reason for that was immediately apparent. Standing directly behind her was her butler, with a massive black umbrella on a wooden pole clasped between his thick dark hands. How he was managing to control the thing in such ferocious winds ought to have been a mystery, but I already knew how solid and immovable the short man was. My gaze went back to his mistress.

She was wearing yet another ankle-length dress, in shimmering black this time and with fine silver filigree across it, that shaped into patterns like the etchings I'd seen on the Plinth. Her feet were bare and caked with mud. Her long black hair was flowing out behind her, pushed there by the raging gale, except that didn't seem to bother her. She was standing tall and proud, her shoulders thrust firmly back. What caught my attention most of all, however, were her eyes.

In the light from my doorway, they seemed a more luxuriant shade than ever. A green that seemed to shift and stir, the way the extreme depths of the ocean might. And two things tried to connect in my mind … the way they looked and that peculiar, puzzling dream I'd had on my first night.

"Are you all right, Mr. Sinclair?"

Her voice broke through my confused thoughts and I struggled fiercely to collect myself.

"I think so, yes. But who were they?"

"We generally refer to them as raiders."

"Seriously? Criminals, you mean?"

"We don't get them very often. Half-breed thugs who skulk around the smaller islands round these parts. They only ever turn up here under the cover of bad weather, and they do it that way to avoid the Coastguard."

"So they came here on some kind of boat, and left in the same way?"

I stared out past her at the raging waves and couldn't even see how that was possible.

"Very expert sailors," she was telling me, "well-practiced in handling storms."

"But how did you know they were coming to my place?"

She was, by this stage, looking horribly proud of herself.

"Fortunately, I was standing by an upstairs window and I saw them cut across the field. It didn't take too much to guess which house they might be targeting."

I let that information sink in and then asked her my most pertinent question.

"But how did you get them to leave? You only spoke a few words and they disappeared."

"They are pagans, Mr. Sinclair, followers of ancient and crude beliefs. I spoke to them in their own tongue—a guttural kind of pidgin-speak—and warned them I would wake their numerous gods and bring the wrath of them down on their heads. And they might be fearsome bandits, yes, but they are deeply superstitious."

One mention of this curious Cthulhu, then, and the whole bunch of them had turned tail and fled? It made sense only in a bizarre kind of way, but I had to admit it had worked. I could feel myself beginning to calm down and took a few much slower breaths before I re-addressed the poetess.

"I reckon I should thank you, that being the case."

"Think nothing of it, Jackson … may I call you that? It would affect me very badly if a neighbor of mine came to harm."

So most of this was centered around her again and very little else … the way that her emotions flowed, the way *she* felt. But, knowing her quite well by now, I wasn't overly surprised by that. My thoughts were progressing on a straighter track now, and I found myself able to turn my mind to matters other than the present one.

"Is Brink still with you?" I asked carefully.

A smile appeared on Anastasia's face.

"He is, and such a charming lad. Many are the evenings we have spent discussing metaphysics and philosophy."

"We're both talking about the same guy? It doesn't sound like that to me."

"One of my most valuable gifts is my ability to draw out people's true potential. To delve beneath the surface and then find the beauty and the truth beneath. You all regarded Brink as shallow, and his fiancée treated him like some kind of lapdog. And so, reacting to those expectations, that is how he acted. But it wasn't who he really was."

Like most things that came out from her mouth, I found it quite hard to believe all this. But I could think of no way I could contradict her without being downright rude, so I pretended to accept what she had said. At which point, memories of another person at the Gorsting house came popping back into my head.

"And your daughter, how is she?" I asked as casually as I could.

Did she even have an inkling of what had transpired that night?

"Ah, yes." And the poetess's manner brightened up. "She told me that she visited you. Quite a while back, wasn't it, and just the once?"

"That's right," I nodded. "Is she well?"

The change that came over the woman's face was so profound it almost shocked me. Gone was any trace of haughtiness or arrogance, and in its place there was a pure delight, so that her cheekbones lifted as she smiled and her sea-green eyes gleamed brilliantly.

"More than well," she almost purred. "Katia, these past few weeks, has begun blooming like a rose."

And with those words, she bade me a good night and headed off, her hair still swirling in the wind and her manservant following with that vast black parasol. I watched them disappear into the storm-wracked shadows, wondering what exactly she had meant by that final remark she'd made.

Katia had been no more than a fragile tepid girl when she had arrived at my door. So what could it be that had turned her into something rather more than that?

CHAPTER TWELVE

THE NAMES OF
THE OLD ONES

i

A man was sent the next day to repair my upstairs window, and he was sent here by guess who. Was there anything about this place that she did not have full and absolute control of? But other than give me the poetess's name; the fellow uttered not a single word. He seemed halfway between a normal human being and one of those Bobsnitch types, very gaunt and sallow-skinned and with protruding eyes, but he went about his job with swift precision and was there and gone in a mere couple of hours.

But beyond that point, the weeks rolled by entirely uneventfully. The weather grew worse, in general terms at least, because there were no further storms and yet the cloud base became denser over Sauquill Island till the light of day carried a funereal tint almost all the time, and there was also a strong fierce wind which simply would not let up.

The Belles of Boston wasn't going well. Anabella Goulding had become a quite peculiar character, prone to utterances that made not the smallest ounce of sense. And I had tried to introduce a minor figure by the name of Berkeley Bradshaw, a simple soul who I believed might provide some real comic relief, but the line between 'funny' and 'sad' is thin and he kept crossing over it.

Mostly robbed of the creative urge which had brought me here in the first place, I turned instead to physical activity, hoping it might clear my mind and so allow my efforts at prose a fresher start. Sometimes I went out for lengthy walks, but for the most part I traveled on my bike, exploring the length and breadth of Sauquill, telling myself that I was on the hunt for inspiration of some kind.

I found precious little, though. The landscape round me stayed impenetrably flat. Murky clouds churned overhead and the cold breeze whistled round my frame. There were largely only isolated homesteads out at the fringes of this place, with no suggestion of motion around them.

But then, almost at the island's north-east tip, I caught sight of what looked like a stone spire up ahead of me and spun toward it eagerly, hoping I had come across some place of interest at long last.

It turned out to be another little church, only the second I had ever come across, similar in structure to the one in Marinsberg, built of blocks of rough gray stone and having very little in the way of windows. But it proved to be derelict too, moss around its mortared joints and wild weeds growing out of them as well. And the front door was boarded up.

Were these a people who'd forgotten God? Or maybe turned from Him to something else, it gradually occurred to me.

On foot and manhandling my vehicle, I went around the back and in that way I came across something I had never been expecting. There was a graveyard to this church's rear, a resting place for this drab island's dead.

But there were no more than a dozen graves in it. And in addition to that fact, most curiously of all, I found myself looking not at simple headstones but at compact mausoleums set above the ground.

Like New Orleans, I told myself, since I had traveled there and partied there a couple of times. But once again, this made no sense. I *knew* why New Orleanians were not buried six feet under—it was something to do with the high water table. Only … why should that be the case here?

I set my bike on its kick-stand and wandered carefully between the blocks. *Jonas Hopkins, 1712-1785* read the inscription on one. *Mary-Anne Deering, 1823-1894. Wilkins McCaul, 1598-1669.* So all of them had been remarkably long-lived for the periods in history that they'd inhabited, and their deaths were set whole centuries apart. I tried to comprehend what I was looking at but could not genuinely fathom it.

There was a cross carved on the tomb of poor Mr. McCaul, but no such symbols on any of the other ones. Instead, there were those swirling hieroglyphs that I had seen etched on the Plinth. Again, I got the strong impression that God-fearing religion had once ruled this place but been replaced by something else.

Who to ask, though? Someone who had lived here a good while, and so my thoughts went almost instantly to Arnold Sewell. And with that idea fixed firmly in my mind, I pedaled hard the whole way back to Marinsberg and parked my bike outside his store.

As I walked in, a shadowy figure moved behind the counter and a face looked up. But I saw instantly this was not him. Instead, it was a man so short that he was practically a dwarf, his head the shape of a slightly flattened orange, pomaded black hair on his scalp, a narrow moustache on his upper lip and very small intense dark eyes. His complexion was rough and colorless, and when he tried to force a smile his teeth looked sharper than they ought. I immediately felt uneasy at the sight of him.

"Can I help you, sir?"

Even his voice was glottal.

"Uh—but where's the boss?" I asked.

"Mr. Sewell? He's gone away. Moved to Hartford to be near some relatives."

"But I was in here just five days ago, and he never mentioned anything like that."

And Sewell had always been a chatty type, not much prone to

withholding information. But the man behind the counter simply shrugged.

"He did it on an impulse maybe, sir. He's never really fitted in round here."

Confused yet again, I managed haltingly to ask him for a fresh batch of cigars. And when he handed them to me, I noticed something else that was odd about this fellow. His hands were decidedly peculiar, the fingers very short, and there appeared to be thin folds of skin between them like the webbing on a frog.

Feeling more than slightly repulsed, I decided to clear my head and so I made my way down to the quay again. It was deserted, not a craft in sight, and even the small line of rowing boats was gone.

Across on the distant mainland, I could see that there was now some cloud cover as well. As though the weather from this place was spreading out and starting to engulf the entire coast.

ii

Some couple of weeks into October—I was not sure quite when, since I had lost most of my track of time—there was another of those wretched 'parties.' Even louder than the rest, hundreds of male and female voices raised against the evening sky, so perhaps the entire population of this isle was there. And the clamor grew more awful as the evening progressed. What started out as heated conversation transformed quickly into shrieks and snarls, voices raised in anger and perhaps in fear, horrid sounds like a baboon might make and I was sure that fighting started breaking out.

The luminous 'artwork' was there once more, denser-looking than ever but at the same time undulating at a faster rate. And the poetess was on her balcony of course, spreading her arms and declaiming, though the racket from below was so intense I could not hear a single word.

It only all died down beyond one in the morning, but I stayed awake for hours after that, realizing that I had come to thoroughly dislike this place and wondering why I had not gone home.

There still had to be some kind of ferry service surely, if only a residual one? The next day—after just a short and fitful sleep—I started off toward the quay once again in the hope of finding out. And I had just gone around the wide bend in the lane and was approaching the dark ugly house when I noticed movement up ahead.

A person was on foot outside the gate and wandering beside the railings. Someone tall and narrow in a beige flat cap and a pair of plus fours.

"*Brink?*" I yelled, and bore down on him rapidly.

He didn't even seem to notice me until I skidded to a halt in front of him. His head was fully lowered but he was doing nothing more than simply shuffling back and forth, like a man who was looking for a lost penny perhaps, or else a man whose mind was gone.

And when his face came slowly up, I almost gasped with shock. It was a pale and hollowed-out visage that I was looking at, the flesh cleaving tightly to the skull, the cheekbones sunken deeply in, the eyes as empty and devoid of life as a pair of seashells on a beach might be.

And there was more than that. The cuff on one sleeve of his coat was torn. There was a fresh-looking split across his lower lip. A faint bruise on his left cheek too. And the index and middle fingers of his right hand had been taped together with a couple of those new-fangled Band-Aid things.

Discussions about metaphysics my damned ass! He kept on staring at me like he wasn't quite sure who I was. I reached across and grabbed him by the shoulders, trying to lift him out of the deep stupor he was in.

"What's been happening to you?" I demanded.

He blinked at me uncertainly, exactly as though he was struggling to understand what I was saying. But then his head went down toward the ground again, and he began mumbling something I could not properly hear.

"What's that?"

"It's not even real," I thought I heard him say.

"*What's* not real, Brink? What are you talking about?"

His face tilted up again. He stared into my own with a lost and haunted look.

"Everything. The entire place. Nothing anywhere is what it seems."

Was he on drugs or was he ill? I was about to press him further in a bid to get some real sense out of him when there was a flurry of activity at the front door of the Gorsting house.

Anastasia came marching briskly out, clad this time in just maroon satin pajamas, velvet slippers on her feet and a huge black robe thrown over all of that. Her hair was tied up in a bulky knot and her face was devoid of any make-up, revealing her as ten years older than she usually seemed. Her lips had formed a stiff line and her glare was steely, even from a distance such as this. And following behind her there was Cuesto once again, still clad at this hour in his uniform.

Brink didn't seem to realize they were coming, and had started stamping gently on the patch of ground that he had been inspecting.

"It's not even real," he mumbled again, like some record with its needle stuck.

"How did you get hurt?" I tried.

I gently took a hold of the hand with the injured fingers, trying to get a closer look at it. And when I did that, Brink's sleeve fell back, revealing yet another wound. There was a bite mark on his wrist, and it looked like a human one. I felt truly shocked when I saw that and wasn't sure how to react.

Anastasia Gorsting finally reached us and she grabbed Brink's elbow, so snatching his arm away.

"Mr. Sinclair, do you take some manner of perverse pleasure from meddling in this way?"

My head was reeling badly, but it was now clear that Brinkley needed my help and so I came back with a strong response.

"We're out on a public street, not inside your home at all, so not intruding. And I've known Brink for many years and I *demand* to know what's happened to him."

The poetess looked affronted at first, but then her features rearranged themselves into an expression close to tolerance, like she had become sympathetic to my grave concerns.

"The party last night …"

"Yes? Go on?"

"One of my own Council members … he got rather badly drunk. And he became aggressive in that state and struck poor Brinkley and he knocked him down. Brink injured his hand when he fell."

"And did the ground rear up and *bite* him too?"

The woman's features froze at that, her green gaze narrowing in upon itself. But then she gave her head a twitch and tried to smile, although she did not manage to do that well.

"I've no idea what you're talking about."

I was about to show her when I noticed further movement near the house's porch. A pale and oval face was peering out, and it was Katia again after all this while.

It made my heart thump to see her. I immediately wondered how she was and what she had been doing since that night. Except that Brink had not been rescued yet, and so I tried to keep him at the center of my thoughts. He was staring at the ground again and prodding at it with one toe, which looked to me like obsessive behavior that was not conscious and was out of his control.

"Do you remember Midge?" I tried.

His brow creased slightly but the motion of his foot did not let up.

"Paris, seriously? And is she still there?"

His leg stopped moving and his face lifted a little way, so I could see his eyes again.

"Your fiancée these past three years? The woman who you used to be completely crazy over?"

His features tightened, hardened up, as though his mind was trying to regain proper traction.

"Midge," he murmured in a low hushed voice. "It really is a shame, what happened."

"To her? What *did* happen to her, Brink?"

Anastasia Gorsting leaned across.

"She decided to part ways with him, partly on account of me, then fell in with a louche artistic crowd who took her off with them to Europe."

"And you know this how? You never met."

"She phoned Brink—a long-distance call."

Except that I remembered—clearly too—that confrontation that I'd had with Midge. She'd tried to phone the Gorsting house, but couldn't even discover the number. What I'd just been told was nothing but an outright lie, and a simmering rage boiled up in me.

"I don't *believe* that she's gone anywhere like that! And *this* is not the man I knew! So what have you people been *doing* to him?!"

There was a swift urgent movement in the corner of my eye which partly brought my focus round. Katia had left the safety of the porch and was now heading across to us.

And there looked to be something different about her, although I could not figure what at first. Like her mother, she was dressed in night attire, a gown in that same white lace and with a coral pink silk robe thrown over it. But she was not moving quite as lightly and as delicately as she had before, and there seemed something a little odd about her general shape as well.

She reached Brink and gripped his other arm, then glowered at me with undisguised hostility.

"Nothing has been done to him. He is a gentle and sensitive soul, and the attack last night unbalanced him. He needs time to recover, Jay, instead of which you're just making him worse."

"Precisely," her mother purred. "Take him indoors, Katia, and look after him."

And the girl nodded, took full hold of Brink and began to turn him round in the direction of the house. I tried to make a move to stop that, but Cuesto took a heavy step toward me and his presence was a threatening one.

Katia had swiveled sideways on, so I was staring at her profile now. And from that angle, I could clearly see what it was about her body that had changed.

She was no longer nearly as slim as she'd been, but showing at the front and obviously with child.

At which point every other thought dropped from my head, and I could only watch numbly as she disappeared with Brink into that wretched residence.

iii

But both of the other two remained in place in front of me, the butler as fathomless as some thick slab of dense hard wood. Anastasia's face, though, had gone through yet another change, like her expressions were only masks which she took pleasure in slipping deftly back and forth. All of her annoyance had evaporated now. Her head was sitting high on an extended neck, her eyebrows had raised up to thin arches of black, and her eyes themselves were glittering with triumph. And the smile upon her lips was a sarcastic, mocking one, like she was thinking of a joke and I was most likely the last line of it.

All the air had left my lungs, my head was blurry and I felt emptied out. In all the years that I had been a bachelor, nothing such as this had ever once occurred.

"In case you're wondering," I could hear the woman saying in a soft but rather cruel tone, "the timing is exactly right, and she has been with no one else."

A vein in my forehead had started pulsing and I jammed my fingers in the corners of my eyes.

"I ..."

"Yes, Mr. Sinclair?"

"Can't she …?"

"Well?"

Miss Gorsting waited for me to go on, except the words would not come out.

"Get rid of it?" she finished up for me. "But my sweet Katia would never end another life."

There are times, thankfully few, in a man's existence when he finds himself totally lost, like he is in some dank and deep-set subterranean cavern and he cannot see the tiniest chink of light. That was how it felt, and I could only think of one direction out. But when I spoke again, I didn't even recognize the sound of my own voice.

"So then … I guess I'll have to make an honest woman of her."

There was utter quiet around me for the next couple of seconds, like the world itself had held its breath. But then that stillness was completely torn apart. The poetess had almost doubled over and was clutching at her narrow ribs; her cheeks were creased up and her jaws were stretched out to their fullest extent. And she was laughing insanely hard, tears running down and spittle spraying from her mouth.

"By all the Lords!" she managed to snort.

Then another wave of hilarity took hold of her for a short while.

"Why, Mr. Sinclair, how very *noble* of you! And how utterly conventional too!"

I hadn't been expecting anything like this for simply trying to do the decent thing, and felt that I ought to be getting angry. But this entire revelation had left me so stunned I couldn't summon up a normal reaction like that.

Anastasia Gorsting finally straightened up again. She shook her head as though to rid it of a fly, and those depthless eyes of hers came fully open at long last. Very damp as they now were, they still managed to stare at me with unhidden derision and contempt.

"Is *this* your solution to the problems that life throws at us? Stand before an altar and surrender yourself to the laws of an unseen and quite unproven God?"

But what was she babbling about now? How did 'proof' come into this? She must have seen how mystified I looked, and she continued eagerly.

"The gods my people worship are entirely real. They can be looked upon and heard and even spoken with."

All humor had left her by this time, and she came rearing up to her full height like some ancient dragon that had woken up.

"Back in the village where I used to live—a little village in the Russian woods, where I was called Gorastovitch—we paid them homage and they answered back, even though they might be half the world away. The Great Ones, yes! The Old Ones, see? Distance—it means nothing to them, as does time. They do not even come from here and they existed long before this world began. Yet one of these almighty beings still decided to choose me."

Before my very eyes, my startled ones, Gorsting seemed to be transforming into something that looked human but was not that thing the slightest bit. Her long-nailed fingers had become sharp spikes that flailed as though to slice the morning air. Her mouth had stretched into a squarish shape so that her exposed teeth looked deathly as a shark's. The rest of her face was rigid as a sculpture, from the depths of which her eyes burned like some bright green furnace out of Hell. I was sure that she was in the grip of some mad, violent seizure and I tried to move away from her, but she stepped forward and kept on.

"He is the mightiest of them all, in fact! Their high priest and soon to be their savior! You have even heard me say His name. It is none other than exquisite, blessed Cthulhu!"

The same name she had invoked when she'd chased those raiders off. But what was this nonsense that she was trying to tell me?

"When I was a tiny girl, He began talking to me in my sleep. And by the time that I was ten, He was conversing with me openly inside my waking head. Guiding me, advising me, taking me down all the paths that would lead me to America and wealth and fame. Every single thing I have

I owe to Him and Him alone. I am nothing but His willing servant and am deeply proud of that."

The sense of shock that I had felt initially was starting to ease off by now and was being replaced by something else. Miss Gorsting here was clearly nuts, as crazy as a turkey in a whole forest of Christmas trees. And more than likely dangerous as well, so I should watch those fingernails and teeth. Except I simply couldn't help myself ... I *had* to ask the question that had risen up inside my consciousness.

"And what is this Cthulhu going to do?"

"Revive the other Old Ones, that is what. Yog-Sothoth and Gol-Goroth, Nyarlathotep and all the rest, who have lain as dead for whole millennia but who can still be returned fully to life. They used to rule this world and they shall rule it yet again, and once they have achieved that goal we human beings shall be free of all laws and morality as well, good and evil meaning naught. And liberated in that way, we shall dance and shout with utter revelry and do whatever pleases us, even kill, and carry out those acts without the slightest breath of conscience, and the entire world shall be seen to burn in a holocaust of ecstasy and freedom!"

Correct what I had said before ... this was all a good long way beyond plain nuts. Utter barking lunacy, and on a level I had never encountered, and I doubted that most people had. Yog-Schm-*what*? Nylon-*who*? She clearly belonged in a padded cell, and only her vast wealth and fame was keeping her from such a place.

She had finished up with her demented rant and was hunched forward all over again, her breath hissing between her teeth and her tall frame quivering. The fire in her eyes had died right down and they looked almost sickly by this stage, so I could finally regard her as she really was— an utterly tormented and unstable creature who had somehow drawn the general public underneath her heinous spell.

My gaze went back to her enormous house, and I finally understood why it had looked to me like some manner of large dark fortress. That was what it truly was, a bastion to keep the rest of the world out. The entire *place* was nothing but a loony bin, with everybody in it trapped like insects in the amber of her bizarre, senseless fantasies. *That* was what those awful 'parties' were about. And simple, cheerful Brink had been sucked in as well.

Her butler was on the move again. He had produced a handkerchief from one of his pants pockets and was mopping very gently at the tide of sweat that had sprung upon his mistress' brow. So it seemed the case that she was very sick indeed, perhaps not merely in the mental sense. I peered at her with something like disgust, then thought *to Hell with all of this* and went away.

There seemed to be no more that I could do for Brink. It made more sense to just get out of here, so I pressed on to Marinsberg again.

CHAPTER THIRTEEN

A TERRIBLE DISCOVERY

i

There was no one at the quay, not even the cab driver, Saul. And all of the storefronts were firmly closed, including the newsdealer's one. And there was not a sound from any of the houses round me—all their drapes had been pulled tight as well. It had just gone seven in the morning by this point, so I waited for a while in the hope that someone might emerge, but it was a forlorn hope.

And not a solitary ship turned up, certainly not the ferry I was hoping for. I could make out the distant shapes of boats moving upon the waves, but they remained tiny and did not come close.

Another thing: the weather, which had been poor for a good long while, had started turning quite considerably worse. This was early in the day and the climate ought to have been warming up, instead of which it was plummeting the other way, getting colder by the minute so that I began to shiver and I turned the collar of my jacket up. Sharp chill gusts had started buffeting at me and seemingly from different directions, and the surface of the sea, affected by all this, was frothing and lashing round.

The clouds above were darker than they'd ever been and lower too, and seemed to be moving over me in a broad, circular, whirling motion.

I could take this no longer, I decided. I was thoroughly confused, chilled to the bone, and quite completely miserable too. And so I pedaled back as briskly as I could, getting my blood flowing again and loosening up my stiffened limbs. I paid scant attention to the landscape as I rode, and when I passed the Gorsting house I turned my gaze away in sheer contempt. At long last, I reached my porch and closed the door of the rented house behind me gratefully.

Except that gratitude did not last long. This place was soundless too save for the moaning of the wind outside and with the lights switched off extremely dim, and it had an unappealing empty feel. What had I been thinking of, spending several months alone in here? I slowly came to realize I had not been thinking all that much, but simply following a routine which had gradually transformed into addicted habit.

Now I'd fully woken up, though, and was able to examine my life as it was and even confront a few facts.

One—I was no novelist. I did not have that talent in me.

Two—I was drinking too much.

Three—my so-called friends had all forgotten about me, and what did that tell me about myself?

And number four and worst of all, I'd let myself get cut adrift from all the trappings of the normal world, and seemed to have become ensnared. I wasn't even sure which date this was, but knew there was a diary in among my stationery. I scrabbled till I found it and then, flicking through its pages, managed to discern that this was later in the month than I had been aware, somewhere around October the 25th in fact.

The wind kept pushing at my outer walls, thrumming at the house as though it were an instrument. The circling clouds grew ever darker out beyond my windowpane, and I felt a deeper form of despair begin to sink over me. Beyond that point, I believe I fell into that kind of melancholic daze where you are not sure what you are doing anymore and lose all track of time as well. When I stared at my watch again, the hands had slipped past the noon hour. I was standing in my kitchen and did not know why. The weather had not lightened up by the slightest touch but continued to seethe and rage and was starting to resemble a mid-winter's storm.

I peered out through my window at the utterly flat field out back. Everywhere I'd gone on Sauqill had been level and I had grown used to that, accepted it. But now I began to re-examine why the island really was this way. And doing so, some words I'd heard came flooding back into my brain

"It's not even real."

Brink had said that just a few hours back, and he had stared down at the ground beneath his feet and even jabbed it with his shoe. But what had he been alluding to?

"Nothing anywhere is what it seems."

My mind started following a different course.

Those mausoleums above the ground, the dead stored there instead of buried two yards down. And when I'd gone to take a close look at the Plinth, I'd stamped on the swathe of rock around the thing and it had a hollow ring.

I had to find the truth of this, and thus impelled I clenched my teeth and went back out into the storm.

There was a small wooden shed against the back wall of the house. Opening it and rummaging through, I came across a shovel, and armed with that I marched to the middle of my small back yard and I began to dig.

To the eyes of any observer who might pass, I had to look like a crazy man, and I was perfectly aware of that. But I concentrated on the task, digging the swiftest hole I could while the elements vented their fury round me. I went down a foot, but came across nothing except damp loose soil. Another foot—some yellow clay came up. I hit a seam of pebbles after that; they slowed me down but they did not deter me.

So I kept on pressing further in until I heard a solid thump. And after that I was not digging anymore but clearing away dirt and debris so that I could properly examine what I'd come across. It took a while to achieve that. The wind kept pushing more grit down, and some of it flew in my face. But finally I cleared a space some two feet wide and took a careful look at what I'd found.

Flat and solid as the deck of any ship, a bare expanse of stone stared back at me. And I recognized it straight away—it was almost jet-black with a greenish tint and with a soapy quality to its smooth surface, and had little golden flecks in it. This was the same mineral that the Plinth was constructed of. And was the entire island based on this?

I stepped across the latticed fence and marched briskly out into the field beyond. And I must have traveled fifty yards before I stopped and tried again. Some more pebbles and clay came up, but then I was rewarded with another stiff, unyielding thud.

The same dark mineral was here again. It had to be lying beneath the entirety of this whole island. So this place was not natural but instead a fabrication. I was struggling to understand what that might mean.

Who—or what—could have constructed such a thing? My bewilderment grew, and with it my sense of trepidation. If Sauquill had not risen in the normal way but had instead been placed here by some outside force, then what purpose did it have? Some kind of trick? Some kind of trap? And I'd been living on the thing for months.

Even worse notions began occurring to me in the next few moments. If anything as utterly unnatural as this could nonetheless be real, exist, then what other dark secrets might this region hold? No mortal power could have ever put this island here, and it had obviously been here for many centuries at least. So could it be the work of paranormal forces then ... even the Great Old Ones that the poetess had spoken of?

Torn apart by dread and doubt, I found myself lurching round until I wound up facing the rear aspect of the Gorsting house.

The poetess herself was out there on the balcony, her long hair flowing in the wind again. And she was peering at me through the lens of her brass telescope.

God in Heaven, but I had to get out of here! I flung the shovel aside and then practically ran back inside the house. Except, once there, I had no further ideas as to where to go. There was no ferry and there were no boats, and this structure was no safe haven—the incident with the raiders had demonstrated that.

And so what was there left for me to do—stop here quietly until Gorsting and her friends all came for me? I was completely on my own and I had brought this on myself, allowing the world to forget about me.

And I was still thinking that very thought ... when my telephone began to ring.

ii

I now realize it was not true that my friends had dropped me from their plans and did not care that I was gone. I found out later on that a good number of them cared a lot, were eager to get in touch and so arrange to visit me. But every single time that their thoughts turned in that direction, their minds would go blank a while, then concentrate on something else.

It was the same as it had been with Esmeralda Ellmans, Lord Cthulhu reaching out and working his telepathic treachery.

But this particular call reached me because the high priest of the Old Ones wished it to.

iii

Desperately, I snatched the handset up, but I was so confounded, so in shock, I could not get a single word out. I was trying but my throat had seized up and the sounds that I was attempting to make could not get past my lips.

"Hello?" came a booming voice. "You there or what? Speak up, Bucko!"

It was a voice I recognized immediately, and no one else had ever called me that.

"Grant?" I managed to gasp out, and with true and heartfelt relief.

"What do you think you're up to, eh?" he almost roared at the far end of the line. "I come back to my old stamping grounds, hoping to look up my favorite bachelor, only to be told he's no longer in Boston. No, he's off playing Robinson Crusoe somewhere, on his own and, at my best guess, living like some kind of schlub. That's not at all like you, Bucko, so what's gotten into you?"

Grant Carrington—exactly like myself—had been born to wealth, but he had struck out on his own and done something with it. He'd founded his own large, successful publishing house, GC Books, then used the movie deals from that to involve himself in Hollywood. But those were not the only things he did. He played polo for the national team. He drove racing cars and flew his own biplane, and his handsome face with its broad moustache appeared regularly in the popular newssheets. He'd been based in Manhattan mostly for the past twelve years, but had been born in Boston and we'd gone through high school side by side.

"Where are you?" was the next thing I asked.

"Boston Harbor, in a hotel by the waterfront. Connie's with me and we came up from New York on the *Verona Fair.*"

Which was one of the three boats he owned, a gorgeous thirty-two foot racing sloop. And Connie was his latest wife, the movie actress Constance Evans, not as well-regarded as a Clara Bow or Louise Brooks but famous for her cool blonde pulchritude. The couple were a fixture at the grandest galas and the most important charity events, and one of the first issues of *Time* magazine had featured them on its front cover, underneath the loud caption 'America's Golden Couple.'

Except my mind was by now fixing frantically upon the fact he had a boat with him.

"Grant, do you know where Sauquill Island is?"

"I've seen it on a chart and passed it a few times. That where you are?"

"The section of the island facing north to Providence. There's a small bay there with a jetty. Could you pick me up from there?"

And by this juncture, Grant was sounding utterly perplexed.

"Try to calm down, Bucko. What's the deal?"

"I think I'm in real trouble, Grant. I can't explain it on the phone, but I badly need to get away from here."

Calm in a crisis as he always was, he paused a moment to turn all this over in his head.

"Connie's off having lunch with friends, but I think I know which restaurant she's at. Get down to that jetty, Bucko, then sit tight. I'll be with you as quickly as I can."

He gave a solemn grunt and then hung up. And merely seconds after that, I was rushing out through my front door and pedaling like Death Itself was after me.

iv

The cold air skimming round my cheeks bit even harder than it had been doing only half an hour back. And the clouds overhead had formed themselves into nearly perfect rings, concentric ones and growing smaller from the outer edge so that the sky above me seemed to have been transformed into some great whirlpool, Charybdis tipped over on its head.

This was not even slightly natural either, so I clenched my jaw and I continued forging on. That wretched house was coming up and there was no way to avoid it. Would its occupants try to stop me leaving, since they now knew what I had found? I peered ahead through the prevailing gloom, but there was no one in the road.

I was standing fully off my saddle by this stage, and in that state of heightened agitation I went past the house in a few seconds. And I tried to fix my eyes ahead, except I simply couldn't help myself. I glanced up past the iron fence, and there at a high window three motionless figures were all staring down at me—Katia to the right, Cuesto to the left, and at their center Anastasia Gorsting. They were motionless as paintings, but I still felt sure their eyes were following me.

Then they were gone behind me and the town was coming up. As before, there was no one about. I paid no least heed to the cobblestones, not slowing down the smallest touch, and was arriving at the quay in record time.

I marched out across the jetty's wooden planks. The weather had become so bad that I could barely see the mainland now, and the sea was rough in a way that it had never been, churning back and forth and making heavy gurgling sounds, like it was caught in some gigantic bowl and an enormous hand was rocking it.

I'd panicked, hadn't I, and had come here far too early on? Grant had told me that he needed to find Connie first, and they might take a while preparing the *Verona Fair* for sail. So I'd be out here in the open for a good while yet, exposed to the elements and heaven knew what else.

I glanced back behind me once again. There was no sign of motion in the whole of Marinsberg, but the circling clouds above the town had dropped still lower, and the center of the vortex which they formed was—by my estimation—directly above Gorsting's house.

Something terrible was on the way. I felt that deeply in my gut. What it could be I had no concept … one of those Old Ones that the poetess had raved about? My world had gone all wrong and had been toppled upside-down, so nothing made sense anymore.

How long exactly would I have to wait? I started walking back toward dry land, then noticed that—where this jetty began—there was a large dip in the ground below, a hollow in the shoreline maybe three feet deep which had more than likely been formed by the eroding tides. And it was wet down there and there was tangled seaweed too, but I lowered myself into that dank space nonetheless. I hunkered down as low as I could manage, staring out at the wild ocean and praying fervently for a sail to appear.

CHAPTER FOURTEEN

THE DENIZENS OF MARINSBERG

i

I glanced at my watch constantly, except that I knew fully well the geography of this seaboard. If the *Verona Fair* was setting off from Boston, it would have to clear the headland of Cape Cod before it could turn west and sail for here, and that would take another while. And the weather would not be helping matters any. It might be hours until help came.

My senses were at full peak, alert for any tiny noise or even a vibration on the ground behind me, the slow rhythm of an approaching tread perhaps, or else the rumble of a wheel. I was filled up with anxious expectation but they did not come, the town remaining quite lifeless behind me.

Yet still I felt that I was not alone, that there was some manner of presence hanging over me. A watching eye and a surveying intellect, totally unseen but studying me. I tried to shake off that idea but could not and it clung to me.

In this little trough that I had climbed into, I was at least in part protected from the wind. The same could not be said, though, for the freezing temperature. I drew my knees up to my chest and did my best to curl into a ball, but it was not sufficient. I began to shake.

My face felt rigid and my teeth were grinding once again. I acknowledged it was hopeless gazing out to sea, and so I let my eyes slide shut.

There wasn't merely darkness back behind them. Everything was once more tinted green, and there were strange shapes outlined in that glow. A giant orb again, and other massive structures set at angles that defied true logic. So was this Cthulhu's home that I was seeing? But I couldn't understand quite how.

A door slid open at a curious angle, and a huge and shapeless face enveloped in writhing tentacles came thrusting out. And I knew it. This was *him*. But how'd a vision of him got into my skull? By very slow degrees, I started to understand it … he had been touching my mind since I had decamped here, that unworldly mental power the poetess had spoken of. And having done that more than a few times, there had to be some kind of psychic link between us.

But I wanted the foul thing right out of my head. I clutched at my temples and I moaned. His tendrils swirled and bubbles rose, but finally his horrid image faded off.

My eyes reopened and the world returned, and it was practically as dark as evening now, but in the middle of the afternoon.

There was still nothing out to sea but lashing waves, colliding and breaking up so heavily that they were practically creating a low fog. But those, unhappily, were the only things I could make out. Not a single craft was on the move out there.

ii

It was well past four when a dot appeared, halfway between this jetty and the coastline off at Little Compton. It was pure white and vanished quickly, so I thought at first that it might only be a breaker's tip. But then it reappeared a couple more times and it was getting closer. I stood up.

Gradually, Grant's sloop bore into view. Its hull was painted white from stem to stern, its decks were of the palest teak, except there were no tall triangular sails visible but rather a bare set of masts, so it was obviously traveling under motor-power.

Two figures were in view on board, both of them in yellow oilskins. Connie was kneeling at the prow and Grant himself was back behind the wheel.

The actress raised herself a touch and waved to me, her famous blonde hair hanging limply down across her shoulders. The poor girl looked soaked right through, so they had had a treacherous journey coming here.

More than fifty yards out from the quay, the vessel slowed down and began to turn. There was a rattle as a small anchor was dropped. And Grant had let go of the wheel by now, had moved to the ship's side and was guiding down a plumb-line.

He studied the result, then cupped both hands round his mouth.

"Bucko, I'm sorry but my keel's too deep! I can't bring us the whole way in!"

So what was I supposed to do?

"Just wait there and I'll be with you in a flash!"

Tethered to the back of the *Verona Fair* and trailing behind it like a new-born pup there was an inflatable dinghy on a length of rope. I watched closely as Grant pulled it in, then clambered down to it and set off swiftly. He rowed with big broad-shouldered pulls and it was not too long before he'd reached the quay and started climbing up. I had left my hidey-hole by this stage and was striding out to greet him.

"Sorry we were so damned long, but these confounded winds keep changing their direction and I couldn't risk using the sails."

He slowed down and stared directly at me, then froze solid, his jaw hanging wide.

"Jay? My *God*, what's been going on with you?"

But I didn't understand what he might be referring to.

"You're pale as a ghost, man. You look ill. And how much weight precisely have you lost?"

That question took me so aback that I stared down at my own arms. My fingers looked like brittle twigs and there were thick veins jutting out on the backs of both my hands. And above my wrists, the sleeves of my jacket were depending loosely. So I hadn't just lost track of time— I'd lost track of *myself* as well, the dark, peculiar spell of Sauquill Island overpowering me.

I began to quiver at that point, realizing how utterly I'd been misled. My throat was choked up and my eyes were filling with hot tears.

Grant saw all that and seemed to understand, and moved swiftly across to me.

"It's okay, Bucko, you're safe now. Let's concentrate on getting you aboard."

And he put am arm around my shoulder, started leading me toward the jetty's edge. Connie was now standing up and watching every move we made.

When suddenly, her focus shifted. She began staring hard at something behind us, and her eyes had gone virtually round with fright.

I could hear a rattling back there, although I couldn't quite tell what it was. But when I craned my neck around, I saw that every front door by the waterfront had now come open and the denizens of Marinsberg were pouring out.

iii

Some were running, but not all of them by any means. Others were taking springing frog-like leaps in the same way the deformed Bobsnitch did. And there were heavy flopping motions too, reminiscent of that stormy night when those three 'raiders' had attacked. So this sudden swift assault did not resemble an attack by any human mob—far more like a mass escape from some unworldly and entirely loathsome zoo.

I could only manage some brief and fragmented impressions of the shapes rushing toward us now. Some of them had broad and elongated feet. Others possessed legs that were most way joined together so they more resembled tails. Some had grossly swollen bellies, others chests in which the ribs stuck out. And there were bulging brows and tentacles for arms and glassy eyes that seemed to have no lids.

And this unholy rabble of debased and corrupted beings—even the more normal-looking ones were grey of face and devoid of expression— descended on us violently. Connie had begun to shriek. Even Grant was rigid for a moment, but he snapped out of that and came to a decision.

"The dinghy! Now!" he blurted out.

And he seized me by the collar, began hauling me toward that goal. And we were on the verge of climbing down, when the water bulged around the edges of the little craft.

There was a sudden heavy ripping sound. A set of claws came tearing upward through the dinghy's bottom and the whole thing began to deflate quickly. Then something dragged its entire structure down and it disappeared beneath the surface with an empty swirl.

iv

The jetty was vibrating now. The hideous crew from the houses was streaming onto it unstoppably, and that first vibration grew until it was a thunder that resounded in my ears.

Gripped by panic, rendered almost senseless by appalling fear, I swiveled back around to be confronted by a sea of deformed faces and unholy forms. And one of them had a straw boater on its head and partially resembled Arnold Sewell, so what had been done to him?

Directly beside me, Grant was standing tall. And he had bunched his fists, and as this vile mob descended on us he began swinging left and right, landing blows on jaws and upper lips that sent our assailants reeling back.

I tried to follow suit but could not match his skill or strength. A tentacle curled round my wrist and hauled me forward so I lost my balance. Other hands closed round me then and lifted me up till I was being carried off at shoulder-height. I yelled out loud and struggled hard, but the creatures paid no heed to me. They simply passed me down along their ranks, and having gotten me the whole way back they flung me to the ground and left me there.

Lying on my side and bruised and shaken up, I was still trying to follow what was going on. The backs of these mutated beings were all turned away. They kept on pushing down along the jetty, going for the man who'd come to rescue me.

And Grant kept fighting furiously, swiping with his fists, lashing with his elbows, even using his knees and his feet. A number of these creatures were quite feeble things and they went down easily beneath his blows.

But one lone man can only do so much, and there were just too many of the debased beasts. They kept on pressing closer until they were all around him and their limbs were clamping round his own. He flailed hugely and he roared, but he was being lifted off his feet as well, as if he were some animal they'd caught.

Another high-pitched scream rang out, and it was coming from the water. My blurred gaze swung across to the *Verona Fair*, to see that lovely Connie was no longer on her own. Dense dark shapes were now emerging from the waves, in the general shape of men except with thicker limbs and darkly gleaming skins and, yes, with overly-large heads, and I had seen these types before. Not human beings but some other race that dwelled in the ocean's depths, perhaps. And they were springing up onto the deck.

She tried to run but there was nowhere to escape. They grabbed her by her ankles and her wrists and dragged her back into the sea. Her head remained above the surface, thank the Lord—she was still yelling out and weeping bitterly. But she was drawn along that way until she made it to the jetty, then surrendered to the grip of the foul mob, who lifted her up as well.

Then all of them were moving off, their two captives still writhing in their grasp. Webbed feet, fused knees and limping legs were going past me in a constant stream. And, light-headed and injured although I might be, I strove to make one final effort. Pushed my shoulders off the ground, and I tried to stand up so that I could intervene somehow.

A heavy foot connected with my chin, and I went down again and everything went black.

CHAPTER FIFTEEN

IN DARKNESS

i

Utter silence, save for a soft lapping over to one side of me. There was no screeching wind any longer, and there was no crashing as from heavy waves. No pounding feet. No screams or shouts. I had not opened my eyes yet. I was bathed in utter silence, save for that soft lapping sound.

Had I died and gone to a dimension where there was no sight? Except my lower jaw was aching terribly, the pain spreading up into my teeth and gums. All my life, I'd never once been hit, let alone been kicked directly in the face. I moved one hand up and I touched my chin. It smarted awfully and I pulled my fingers back.

And realized how cold they were, so plunged into iciness they kept on trying to curl up and I was unable to hold them straight. And the same seemed to be true of my whole body—I was curled into a fetal ball, my spine an arc and my knees bent.

How had my environment turned so wintery so fast? Uncertainly and by small increments, my eyelids stretched themselves apart.

To be rewarded with the picture of an almost static scene. I was facing the jetty once again, and the ocean around it had gone practically flat, nothing more than little wavelets dappling its surface now, which accounted for that lapping sound. The jetty itself was completely empty, as though nothing in the slightest part had happened there. And the *Verona Fair* was still where Grant had left it, bobbing softly on the placid tide. The sky off in that direction was cloudless and entirely clear, the stars and a half-moon shining down, although they had that frosty nimbus round them which sometimes becomes apparent on extremely cold nights.

I managed to sit halfway up. My neck hurt too; it felt as if it had been bent at a sharp angle and had gotten stuck in that position and my shoulders were uncomfortably tense. But I ignored all that and swung my upper body round to take another look at Marinsberg behind me.

All of the front doors were still wide open but I could not see a single light. The place looked like a termite hill that had been deserted by its crawling bugs. So where had the inhabitants all gone?

My gaze went higher, above the clustered rooftops, and I sucked in a sharp breath. The circling clouds up there had contracted to a solid disc, perhaps only a hundred yards in width and positioned directly above the Gorsting house. And it was churning and billowing, yes, only it kept on spinning too, whirling like a mighty wheel and at ferocious speed. And how could that be happening in the absence of any wind?

But then a singular reality came rushing back at me with urgent force. Grant and Connie in the clutches of that horrid crew? And more than likely captives of the poetess as well? I stared round wildly, looking for my bike, but it was nowhere to be seen. So, taking little notice of the sheer discomfort I was in, I pushed myself the whole way to my feet. And once my balance had returned, I started out across the cobblestones.

ii

The atmosphere around me was completely still, and there were patches on it of that strange translucent mist you sometimes get on winter's nights, thin and disembodied as a scattering of ghosts and eerie-looking in the way they hung about. And the windows round me were all etched with frost—I went by them as quickly as I could, although I didn't have the strength to run. My body was so deeply chilled that I felt lucky to have woken up at all. My limbs were shivering and rigid simultaneously, but I kept rubbing at my arms and I continued to move onward with my condensed breath pluming before my face.

When I reached the edge of town, the lane was stretching out ahead of me, the open countryside beyond it moveless as a chunk of lead. Even the trees' branches here were glittering with frost, but this was just October and it was not in the least natural.

I craned my neck back awkwardly again. The disc of cloud above the house was spinning even faster and that startled me and I pressed on.

Never in my whole time here had I traveled the entire length of this path on foot, and in the weakened and ungainly state that I was in it seemed a Herculean task, the unpaved track reeling endlessly ahead of me, the trees which lined it going past me one slow shadow at a time. But I did not give up and I persisted trenchantly. My friends had put themselves at serious risk to come here and try to help me, so what kind of man was I if I didn't attempt the same for them?

Even the ground beneath my tread was covered up with hardened frost. Ice gleamed between the pebbles there and crunched under my every step. And that transfixed me for a while; my brow was lowered as I plodded on. But then I realized there was something brand-new happening overhead.

There was a sudden heavy thud of beating wings. I tried to make out what was causing that, but a tree was in the way and by the time I'd passed beneath its limbs the source of the noise had disappeared. It must have been something large though, or I would not have heard it so clearly.

Considerably higher up, something flashed against the backdrop of the stars. I tried to track it with my gaze, but that was hard since—whatever it might be—it was as dark as the night itself and largely blended into it. All that I genuinely managed to get was a vague impression of an undulating motion, that and an impression of unnaturally large wings, but then it faded and was gone.

But what *were* these? There seemed to be two of them at the very least. My heart was beating faster now, forcing warm blood through my frozen limbs. And that had the effect of loosening me up, driving the appalling stiffness from me so I started moving at an easier pace. And fresh adrenaline was accompanying that, charging my whole body with a renewed, vital urgency. I kept the Carringtons fixed in my thoughts and pressed forward with new-found vigor.

Before much longer, I was practically beneath the disc of cloud. And something moved across its pale expanse; there and gone in just a bare couple of beats. But I could nonetheless discern its general shape—it seemed to be nearly all wings, and not those of a bird but of the bat-winged type, composed from stretched-out jagged membranes. Of the creature's body I could make out nothing much, save that it was slender and you could not make out any head. And I'd seen such a winged beast my first night here, when I had woken from that dream.

Another one appeared, and then two more. They started circling high above the house like something down there was attracting them. But from this great distance, I could not tell how large they were or what kind of threat they might present.

What dragged my attention off from them was a sudden clattering and grinding sound—up ahead of me and down here at ground level—from some unseen source along the path. This lane was so enfolded in black shadow, though, I could not fathom what was making it at first.

Then something came emerging out of that deep gloom and I could see that it was moving at great speed. Something very large and quite bizarre, devoid of any proper form. There were two huge long heads right up at the front of it, both of them with flat bared teeth and rounded eyeballs that were mostly white. Behind those were large bodies with long legs, but moving so fast they were impossible to count. And behind all of that there was a shapeless mass which squealed and rumbled and was throwing off bright showers of sparks. I was so dumbfounded by this sight that I was frozen to the spot.

But then, as it drew closer—and it did that very quickly—I figured out the truth of this. It was a pair of horses I was looking at, teamed together by their harnesses but both of them possessed with mindless panic. And the object to their rear was the carriage they'd been tethered to, but tipped over on its side, being hauled along and torn to bits.

I was so astonished that I barely managed to react in time. As the steeds and their burden rushed at me, I flung myself out of the way. And not a moment too soon either. Eight beating hooves went thundering past, and as the carriage followed one of its rear seats broke off, bouncing and then spinning through the air and coming very close to hitting me. But then the whole ensemble vanished in the murk, although I could still hear it and its blazing sparks could still be seen.

Badly shaken all over again, I forced myself slowly up. I was almost at the house by now, and further chilling noises were emerging from its grounds.

iii

The maddened shrieks and wails that I could hear were clearly being produced by other horses, and by the sounds of it a number of them too. But other ugly brays were now reaching my ears, and of a type that I'd become extremely familiar with.

That wretched building finally came in view, like some vast obsidian gravestone against the dimness of the night. All its windows were lit up, and their glow illuminated the sheer chaos in the courtyard at the front.

It was full of carriages and carts, almost more of them than it could take. Most of them were overturned as well, and as for their unfortunate beasts, they had been driven wild with fear, kicking and rearing and screaming.

A few more lucky ones had managed to break free. And the gate was wide open—as I watched, three skinny steeds found their way through then raced away across the flattened ground. But all the rest were firmly trapped.

The carriages in there were being kicked to bits. Hooves were flailing wildly through the air and coming down on unprotected flanks. But there were reports from human throats as well.

They were those whoops and howls and other guttural sounds I'd heard from this house previously, but amplified incredibly this time, like every single soul who lived on Sauquill had shown up. And that suspicion was confirmed when I moved closer to the railings and could see dozens of bicycles piled up against them. Others, doubtlessly, had traveled here on foot.

There were also sounds of destruction emerging from the house itself. Glass and pottery and woodwork being smashed, and what in God's name could account for that?

But Grant and Connie had to be in there as well, a fate awaiting them I could not even start to guess at. The front door was halfway open, only there was no way through. Try to make my way past all those frantic steeds and I'd be battered and then struck down by their hard sharp hooves.

But a couple of the carts were still upright, and one of them was standing just a few yards from the gate. Taking a deep breath, I flung myself in through the gap, dropping to my knees and slithering along till I was underneath the metal framework, big spoked wheels protecting me.

I made it to the front edge on my hands and knees. Another upright carriage proved to be no further than four yards away. Bracing my whole body, I charged forward at high speed but was careful to keep myself low. And thank heaven I remembered to do that—a pair of flailing hooves went by a few inches above my neck. Had I been standing any taller they'd have struck my head.

The structure I was under now was one of the much larger carts, and so I ought to have felt safer there. But it was still attached to a team of four and being hauled from side to side, and the flanks of other crazed horses were thumping up against it constantly. This was like being inside a kettledrum, the whole frame shaking just above my head, and the stink of equine sweat was thick down here and I was struggling to catch my breath.

And maybe I had stranded myself too. The next upright carriage was two yards along and should have been easily reached, but as I watched a massive roan went slamming fiercely into it. It tumbled over twice and broke in half, so there was now no cover left.

I glanced across my shoulder, only to make out the first cart I had hidden beneath was being smashed to pieces too. So I had no way up ahead and no way back. And I was starting to despair, when suddenly the mood of all the horses changed.

They went still and fell quiet a moment, something new capturing their attention. But next moment their shrieking started up again, and it was even higher-pitched. They were not rearing on their hind legs any more but moving frantically and all in one direction, toward the tall fence which surrounded this place. They forced their foam-streaked bodies up against the solid iron railings. Some even tried, quite futilely, to scramble over them. I eased my head out and peered up, and got a glimpse of what was causing this.

Several of those bat-winged beasts had swooped right down, were circling the house's roof, and the steeds were clearly petrified of them. But it still took my half-numbed mind a few more seconds to grasp the chance that had been given me.

This section of the courtyard was completely clear. I sprang up to my feet once more, and it was no more than a few more hurried striding steps till I was in.

CHAPTER SIXTEEN

Insanity And Revelation

i

There were people on the move in here—not as many as I had expected from the great profusion of vehicles outside, but enough to fill the first floor of the house with violent activity. And as I had guessed from the racket they were making, they had set about destroying every item in this place. Crockery and porcelain and glass lay broken up across the entire floor. The furniture had all been smashed and torn to its component parts. Somebody, or more likely several souls, had managed to tear down the chandelier and it was lying tilted to one side, gleaming crystal droplets scattered all about.

And the islanders who'd carried out this wanton destruction were still at work, breaking all the windows now and even kicking holes into the plaster of the walls. A few of them had the deformities I'd taken note of earlier on, but most of them were largely human, although of a degraded sort. Their backs were bowed, their faces wrinkled prematurely. There was no color to their flesh or any luster to their eyes, like they had spent their whole lives in ghastly, brutal servitude.

I caught sight of the Chinese maid. She had a butcher's knife in one gnarled fist and she was moving up and down the room attacking all the paintings, even the rarest and most valuable ones, slashing at the canvases then tearing the frames down and shattering them between her hands.

"Art is form!" she was yelling, "and from this point onward there shall be no more of that! No structure and no rules, and we shall live our lives in ecstasy and freedom and pure revelry!"

I waited for them to notice me … to get the fact that I was not one of their number and then turn on me with equal violence, but they didn't seem to realize I was there. They just continued with their mindless mayhem, not a single gaze being directed at me, and I went past them quite unharmed.

The Carringtons were nowhere to be seen, and neither was the poetess, so I went charging up the stairs, taking them three at a time until I'd reached her study. It turned out that that room was empty too, except the vandals had been there and they had done a very thorough job. The desks and chairs and even the easel were all smashed to matchwood now. Gorsting's paintings had been ruined too, and every single book had been pulled down and ripped into confetti, wisps of paper everywhere. And the destroyers hadn't stopped at that—the parquet flooring was torn up.

Out on the broad balcony, past the broken French windows, both the table and the telescope were gone. And there was *still* no sign of anyone, but I went out there all the same.

And I looked down.

And froze again.

ii

Outdoor lights on tall metal posts had been switched on down there, the same sort of Victorian streetlamps that I used to wander past on Boston Common. And in their sickly ochre glow, a great mass of humanity—and even sub-humanity—was seething through the grounds, moving not as one but individually so that the chaos down there was intense. Some were leaping up and down, or whirling round, or lashing at the air, shapeless cries arising from their mouths.

And we shall dance and shout with utter revelry, as the poetess had said.

Others, though, were interacting, although not in any pleasant way. Men, women and creatures unidentifiable as such were brawling, clawing, kicking and biting. I watched as one smaller man was beaten to the ground and stamped upon. A teenaged girl jumped on another woman's back, then sank her teeth into her victim's carotid, resulting in a spurt of blood.

This was how Brink had been hurt! How Gorsting had lost a finger and an eye! I was staring down upon the darkest of all bacchanals, devoid of any joy, bereft of even the thrill of carnality, but given over to a type of brutish cruelty the like of which I'd never witnessed.

And we shall do whatever pleases us, even kill, and do those things without the slightest breath of conscience

Bobsnitch and his fellows were all down there too. And I spotted, once again, the thing that had been Arnold Sewell. But then I caught a glimpse of Brink himself. There was blood smeared across his face except he didn't seem to notice that. He had a younger fellow by the throat and was trying to strangle him. He looked completely lost in that foul act, and I had no doubt that he was lost to us.

My other friends were still not in plain view, but it was none of that which caused me to freeze up. Rather, it was what this maelstrom of violence was wheeling round.

When I'd stood out here before, and when I'd looked down at the grounds below, I'd seen only a stretch of lawn but with a slightly elevated bulge. But now it was quite clear how thoroughly I'd been deceived, the truth hidden from me by Cthulhu's powers.

There *was* no grass and no slight bulge. Instead—and I could scarcely believe what I was looking at—there was a massive dome constructed of a dark lusterless kind of metal.

It looked impenetrable in the lamplight. And when a reveler or fighter crashed against it, it rang with a hollow sound. There were inscriptions on its surface, yes, those alien-looking symbols I had looked at several times earlier on. And halfway across there was a straight indented line, which pointed to the notion that it had two halves.

What a perfect *fool* I'd been! How could I have been so wholly tricked?

From beneath that dome, a sudden awful noise rang out. A dreadful empty booming clamor such as might be made by blowing on a conch, but vastly louder than just that. It rose up in intensity until the very air vibrated and the balcony shook, and I was forced to clamp my hands across my ears.

The mob below had gone entirely still, as though this was a signal that they recognized.

The dome shuddered gently then began to creak, and the indented split grew wider.

It was opening up.

CHAPTER SEVENTEEN

THE HORRORS OF THE TEMPLE

i

As the paired halves of the dome slid back and disappeared into the ground, a secretive space was revealed to me that answered two descriptions simultaneously.

First, it was a pit, but not a pit of any natural kind. Its rounded walls were absolutely smooth and described the same precise circle as the metal covering had done. And, perfectly symmetrical and regular, it sank into the soil—if you could even call it that—some thirty feet or so, practically the depth of three stories of an apartment block. Its walls and its flat floor were of the same blackish-green soapy stone I had found out to be the basis of this isle and they glittered in the same way too, with tiny flecks of gold.

But in the second place, it was apparently some kind of temple, although not to any normal god. There were those same alien inscriptions on the walls and floor, but there were other curious features too. At the center of that rounded space, set on a thick upright stem, was a large metal cone with short lenses protruding from its flattened top, and I'd seen newspaper depictions of such an object a while back. It was a projector of some type, built for something called a 'planetarium,' only that that device—as I recalled—was housed in Germany, so how had Gorsting managed to get hold of one?

Back past that there were two far larger objects that appeared to have no commonality with science. Two thick columns of the same peculiar stone, exactly squared-off to a four-foot width and rising maybe eight feet high. It was the carvings at the top them, however, that sent a sickened quiver through my frame. The same monstrous creature was depicted twice, and I definitely recognized its face.

Squatting down upon on all fours, its thick fleshy body was slug-like and vile, but that was not the worst of it by any means. Massive curving talons were protruding from the extremes of its hands and feet, far longer than those of any animal that walked upon this world. A pair of wings was folded up against its back, not like the ones that I had seen above this house but greatly more like dragon's wings. And yet it was the visage of the creature that appalled me most … a squid-like face and covered with long tentacles. Precisely the same as I had seen in that first dream, and then in several visions after that.

Was this the 'priest' that Anastasia had spoken of, Cthulhu himself?

So deeply embedded was the pit that it should never have been possible to make out all of this so clearly. But the dark green stonework looked like it had somehow come alive. The little golden flecks in it were shining with a fervid brilliance, as though some unknown source of energy was coursing through their scattered expanse.

But then I picked out something else. There were some arches in the temple's walls, in the same manner that you might look upon in an ancient Roman coliseum. So there was more to this whole structure than the naked eye revealed, more hidden and mysterious areas tucked away back there.

And in those spaces, I could see, dim shadows were on the move.

ii

They joined together, thickened, coalesced, until they formed one solid mass of moving gloom. I found myself tensing up with apprehension, wondering what was going to emerge.

A horde of upright figures came abruptly surging out, at least three dozen of them, maybe more. And I could see immediately that they were among the most deformed ones of this entire group, flippers in the place of limbs, hard spiked ridges down some backs, and a couple of these beasts even had faces that were bearded with thin tentacles, and those tendrils were moving independently.

But they were dragging along a different figure in between them, and a far more normal one as well. They had it by both its arms, so it was stretched out as though captured on a rack. I could not see its face but I could make out long hair trailing down.

Connie Carrington? But surely not. It was hard to tell in this strange filtered light, but the swaying locks that I was gawking at seemed to be of a far darker hue.

Whoever it was—and it was probably a she—was hauled past the projector and placed firmly in between the two pillars. Then several of the mob were reaching up ... it turned out that a pair of matching silver chains was attached to the stonework, and with manacles at both their ends. The creatures fastened those around the wrists of their captive and then stood back.

And the figure so revealed ... it turned out to be Katia they had trapped this way. Her slender and coquettish form and long black hair were in clear view. And she was dressed in white again, though not in any manner earlier seen but in the form of an extremely brief pearlescent gown that barely reached down to her knees.

She did not try to fight against her bonds. The girl appeared to be enfolded in some kind of trance, her chained arms stretched out to the sides as if she had been crucified. Her head was lolling down across one shoulder with the eyes half-closed, the lashes slack. My heart had leapt into my mouth. Had she been drugged or had her mind completely gone?

The hideous beings who'd secured her all moved back against the temple's walls, and they did that with such a slow and solemn gravity it left me with the strong impression that some kind of ritual was underway. Once that they were all in place, the projector burst into life, its lenses whirling round and shining. Some of them glowed a deep dirty blue and others still a leprous green, so that that curious 'artwork'—a mix of both—was thrust high up in the air again, the hues pulsing and rippling.

The disc of cloud above became heavily infused with that same glow. The eye of it had moved directly over us. I did not know what that might signify, but did not fasten my attention up there for too long. No, it snapped back to Katia again.

The bright light had revealed the vulnerable condition she was in. The gown that she had on was not merely pearlescent, it was diaphanous too, and bathed in this cyanic glare the outline of her body could be made out clearly, including the swollen part.

Chained up like that, she was the epitome of the word 'helpless.' Was she going to be turned into a sacrifice ... was Anastasia insane enough to do that to her own daughter, and while the girl was with a child? I leant out across the balustrade, my entire body quaking, and I tried to think how I could make this stop.

But then there was a movement in another darkened arch, and the poetess herself stepped through.

iii

She was proudly upright once again but I had never seen her move so stiffly and unnaturally, like I was no longer looking at a human being but at a machine formed in the shape of that, the face built out of porcelain perhaps, so deathly pale her cheeks and brow were.

Little of the rest of her could be made out. She had on another neck-high dress, fashioned from black satin this time, which reached down to her wrists and down below her ankles, and she had a pair of black gloves on.

A curious shimmering rose from the fabric she was wearing, and I saw next moment it was heavily etched with threads of silver too, plastered with those alien symbols top to toe.

There was more movement from that same arch, the butler Cuesto in his habitual uniform and following his mistress out. His elbows were tucked up against his sides, his forearms pushing out ahead of him, and resting on his upturned palms was a black satin pillow.

Lying on it was a long curved dagger, its blade gleaming with fresh-honed metal except with its handle black.

I realized the point had come at which I had to intervene somehow. It was too long a drop down to the ground from here, and so I span around and got back to the stairs and began rushing down.

iv

I could hear the poetess's raised voice as I pushed on through toward the back. She was yelling hoarsely but I only caught brief snatches of it. Something about 'cosmos.' Something about 'stars' as well. I thought I picked out 'Old Ones' too.

I burst into the open air, and there were hundreds of turned backs between myself and the temple, a wall of silhouetted figures, each of them as still as though they had been sculpted there. There was no choice but to begin forcing my way through. Not a single one of them reacted to my doing that. Their bodies remained rigid and they cast not so much as a small glance at me. Their gazes and their rapt attention were fixated on the poetess.

I finally made it to the edge. Gorsting was standing next to the projector now, her frame bathed in that pulsating light, her head tipped back and her arms raised above her head, and she was crying out with genuine passion.

"The stars are in their right alignment! Travel between them is now possible!"

There was a maddened delight in her eyes and an expression close to

❧ *161* ☙

rapture on her face. But who might be traveling, and how?

"She has awoken fully! She sees us and She comes here from the darkest, coldest hollows of the Universe! Cthalhia, bride of Cthulhu, joined to Himself not in love—for the Great Old Ones know none of that—but linked to Him by way of divine destiny, an omnipotent wholeness which They will form once joined! An even greater power, yes! An even mightier intellect combined! And They shall rule together and shall free us from the laws of men, and this whole world shall dance and howl and burn with joy!"

Katia's head had lifted just a little, though her eyes were still completely glazed, so dark they looked like chips of polished ebony, so I doubted she could fathom what was going on. I started to move along the temple's edge, looking for some way that I could get down into there. Once again, it was too steep a drop to manage with a jump, only there had to be an entrance to this place somewhere. I cast my gaze about but could not see a hint of one, so it was obviously a hidden one.

Gorsting senior had turned away and was moving slowly to the pillars now, her butler matching every step. And was she going to slaughter her own child? My pace sped up frantically.

Anastasia swung round again, her arms spreading to the sides this time.

"Cthalhia must be honored when She arrives here! We must greet Her with an offering, and it must rightly be blood!"

I was almost running now, going round in circles like a rodent on a wheel, but I still could not discover any entranceway.

"And it should be," Gorsting was screeching now, "a human of significance and his fair bride!"

Which stopped me dead, my feet hovering on the temple's rim, since I had a strong suspicion of what those words might mean.

Another crowd of deformed and mutated figures pushed out into view down there, perhaps a hundred of them this time round. And high above their heads, two supine figures were being borne, one of them with long blonde hair, the other tall and with a broad moustache.

v

Barely conscious as they were and trapped for hours in the creatures' clutches, Grant and Connie had both been abused. Their oilskins and their shoes were gone. Their clothing was ripped and there were fresh and livid bruises showing on their skin.

Neither of the pair was trying to free themselves. Connie looked to be in shock, her gorgeous face completely slack and her blue eyes as vacant as twin pools of ice, not fastening on anything. As for Grant, his chin was purple-red where it had been struck several times and he looked most of the way out of it.

And this was simply just too much. Perhaps, if I clung on with both my hands and lowered myself fully before letting myself drop, then I could make it to the temple floor. I got down on my knees and started trying that, but that caught Anastasia's attention and her gaze went immediately to me.

She didn't lift a finger, she just signaled with her eyes. And instantly, four figures round me came alive, reaching down and pulling me back up, then holding me in an inhumanly strong grip. One of them, I was appalled to see, was Brink himself, his body as stiff as a mannequin's might be and his face entirely blank.

Once that I had been secured, the poetess ignored the fact that I was there, returning her surveillance to the Golden Couple in her grasp.

"Fasten them well now! Fasten them *tight*!"

Grant and Connie were both moved apart and then set upright on their feet, their backs against the two stone pillars. And I noticed in that moment that there were not only silver chains attached. Fastened to the front of each there was an iron ring, fastened well above a person's natural height. Leather cords were produced from the mob. My friends' arms were shoved above their heads, and then two of those Bobsnitch types went scuttling up and fastened their wrists to the metal loops.

Connie's head dropped forward slackly, except Grant was beginning to come around. For myself, I was still struggling against my captors' clutches but I couldn't free myself a little bit.

I could only watch with stark dismay as Anastasia took the dagger from the pillow, lifting it toward the clouds above.

"Beloved Lady Cthalhia, accept this homage that we make to You! Not merely the spilling of fresh blood but the snuffing out of two fine lives, though meaningless compared to Yours!"

So *this* was the true source of the screams I'd heard when there had been a 'party' at this place. That missing redheaded girl ... Helen James, I thought her name had been? And even Brink's fiancée, Midge? And had he stood and watched that happen? Absolute horror washed over me and I was yelling fiercely by this point, though no one took the slightest notice. Tears had begun streaming down my cheeks.

Gorsting started moving in on Grant. Sensing the peril that he was in, his eyes blinked and came fully wide. He took in the woman and her weapon in one glance, then tried to look above his head, clearly wondering why his arms were trapped. And once he'd ascertained the plain reality of it, he set his teeth, strained mightily against his bonds, but the leather cords just would not give.

The poetess was almost on him now. I could see Grant's mind working quickly and he did the only thing he could ... he raised one leg and tried to push her away with his foot.

But the poetess's response was just as swift. She lashed down with her knife hand and she drove the dagger deep into the soft flesh of his thigh.

Grant's face shriveled up with agony, only that didn't last for very long. Gorsting was now springing on him like a spider darting to the center of its web, ripping his shirt open and then driving the blade in again, and it went through his heart this time.

I'd stopped shouting out, I think. Or else I'd gone completely deaf, because the world around me seemed entirely hushed, not the tiniest sound remaining in it by this time. The disc of cloud still whirled above, the stars still glittered beyond that, but the scene below me was devoid of noise.

Then that was broken by a scream, a loud and deeply piercing one. Connie had finally come back to her senses—perhaps it would have been far better for her had she not. She was staring wildly at her husband, whose arms were still stretched above his head, except the body below them lay slumped, blood staining his shirtfront and all the life gone from his vibrant frame.

The gorgeous young woman looked like she'd returned to consciousness only to find herself inside some kind of waking nightmare, and indeed that was the truth of it. Her blue eyes were stretched insanely wide in a face frozen solidly. Spastic jolts were running through her frame, like she was in the grip of a powerful seizure. And her screams went on and did not cease till Gorsting casually stepped across, then lashed out with the blade again and severed Connie's throat.

I felt like I'd left my body. Like I'd floated up from it and was now watching all of this from several miles above. Two handsome, charming, much-admired people … they had been alive a few seconds ago, but now they had been turned to lifeless husks, their blood pooling thickly on the temple floor. Who were these Old Ones that they took satisfaction from this mindless, pointless type of murder?

I got the feeling I was going into shock myself and tried to struggle against that, letting anger fill me up instead. And I pulled against the hands restraining me but still couldn't manage to break loose.

At which moment, something else occurred to me. If Grant and Connie were the sacrifices, why was Katia in manacles? Why had she been chained at all?

My gaze went back to Anastasia Gorsting, who had surely planned every last move of this. A grin had sprung up on the woman's face that could only be described as blissful. Her demeanor had taken on the lightness of a girl-child, every movement delicate and breezy like this was the finest moment of her life. My friends were dead and she was reveling in it—I could now see what evil looked like in its truest form.

She was moving in on Katia by this juncture, with the gore-drenched dagger clasped in both her hands. The girl had still not woken fully up and was only watching this through half-closed eyes.

Anastasia stopped in front of her and then removed the glove from her right hand. She ran her index finger up along the blade till that digit was covered with blood. Then she reached down and began to trace a symbol on the fabric covering Katia's swollen front.

A broad circle at first. Then, inside that, something resembling an inverted pentagram, but with far too many lines and with curious wavering appendages as well. And once that she had finished it, the poetess spun around and faced her disciples triumphantly.

"Behold!" she howled. "I've placed upon my own daughter a mark the world has never seen! But soon the world shall know it all too well … the Symbol of Cthalhia!"

Her eyes clamped shut the next instant and she swayed gently on the spot, her lips pressed together and her brow furrowed with concentration, as though she was sensing something the others could not. And then the whole length of her body jerked. Her head whipped back on a distended neck so she was gazing straight up at the sky.

"*SHE FINALLY COMES!*"

There was a hollow click as the projector was switched off. And when the lightshow disappeared, the temple was plunged into a depthless murk in which almost nothing could be properly made out. Which left me with little choice but to stare directly up myself. The whirling disc had started growing brighter.

Something from above was lighting it up, only how could that even be? There was *nothing* up above it but the empty atmosphere, and beyond its far limit just the cold and hollow vacancy of space. But had something journeyed to us from out there? My captive frame went absolutely stiff.

The circling clouds grew brighter still, but it was not a white light I was looking at. No, this was a bluish-green, the self-same color the projector had brought into being, though considerably more intense. It hurt my eyes to look at it; there was a sheer ferocity to that atrocious glare which spoke of power beyond anything we humans knew. A kind of brilliance the gods might summon up, and demons too. I held my breath.

Next moment I was almost blinded, since a coruscating beam of light—and of the exact same hue—came lancing down from the eye of the vortex, filling the whole temple with its searing glow. Everyone down there apart from Katia dropped immediately to their knees, and all the figures round me too. Which meant that their hands dropped away and so I was no longer being held, but all I managed was one small step forward, so wrapped up in awe was I.

Where *was* this Cthalhia beast? I'd been expecting some monster to arrive, all tendrils and grasping claws and with a savage visage out of my worst dreams. Instead of which, there was nothing but this light. Just a color, that was all. And what harm could a color do?

Anastasia Gorsting finally put down the dagger. Hunkered on her knees like all the rest, she was gazing from side to side and her features were suffused with utter joy. She let out a delighted laugh and raised her palms toward the beam.

"Welcome, Lady! We are deeply honored by Your presence here! We devote our bodies and our souls to You and Your omniscient Lord, for we are happy to be nothing but Your willing slaves!"

This to a color? To a light? I couldn't make the slightest sense of it and stood there nearly witless, trying to understand. Until the shaft of cyan brilliance started to contract, that was.

It withdrew from the temple walls and gradually drew inward to a tighter ray, and it glowed still brighter as it managed that, its luminosity condensing to almost a solid rod. Which slid across the stone floor, leaving all its worshippers to kneel in darkness until just one shape was still lit up.

Burning as intensely as some blue-green sun, the glow had become concentrated around Katia. Her head had come up by this stage and she was looking round like she was not sure where she was.

The glow seemed to push into her slim and sylph-like body and then fill it up. The girl was shining bluish-green as if she'd been transformed into some kind of lantern. Her eyes were rounded, puzzled-looking, as was her wide open mouth, and so it seemed she didn't understand what was happening to her.

And then the light began to pulse, the beat of it so horribly intense it assaulted my optic nerves. I was only catching brief glimpses of Katia now. She'd tipped her head back and begun to shriek.

The violent strobing quickened up, the entire temple and surrounding rim blasted into shattered fragments by its ever-mounting frequency, like watching a spool of film that was being run at much too fast a speed, the actress at the center of it vanishing and reappearing. And it looked like Katia was in agony by now, tossing her head furiously and tugging at her chains and wailing like she was on fire. And that—before my sickened gaze—turned out to be partially the case.

Her skin had started bubbling up in places, as if flames were being applied. Her face was creased up in a ghastly way and parts of it were turning black. Her eyes now had a blind internal glow, like fire had gotten in them and was eating its way out. Her flesh began to smolder and some smoke arose. I'd never heard anybody howl in pain like that.

And I was thinking I could stand no more of this, when suddenly the pulsing stopped. The beam of light vanished altogether, snapping off as rapidly as it had come. Katia was no longer moving, reduced to a small charred shape which just hung there between the outstretched chains.

Then it began to fall apart, fragments of her body dropping to the floor, hitting it and crumbling to dust. Before much longer, she was gone. But there was something lying in her powdery remains. A huddled shape, small and largely oval. So ... the child that she'd been carrying, maybe?

It was too dark down there to really tell, only its general shape did not seem right.

And then a tentacle came flopping out.

CHAPTER EIGHTEEN

ARRIVAL

i

Anastasia Gorsting laughed again. But the next moment—still down on her knees—she was being forced to scramble back, because the creature up ahead of her had started growing larger, and was doing that at a horrific speed.

It was swelling immensely and in seconds too, bulging outward in the self-same way a hot-air balloon might rapidly expand. More tentacles came lashing out, and they were attached to its face, the same way I had witnessed in my visions and my dreams.

Wings like those of some fantastical dragon were unfolding from its back, precisely as depicted on the statuettes. Its limbs were blunt and very thick, and each one terminated with a set of claws practically the length of sabers and impossibly sharp-looking too. Its three tiny eyes, between the tendrils, were a bilious green, had an internal glow, but also had a definitely intelligent and watchful look, like they were drinking in their new surroundings, taking careful stock of them.

The thing was spreading out to fill the whole circular space down there, had already risen to perhaps twelve feet and was expanding to the sides as well. The two pillars were still in its way, but the strength of their hard stone proved to be no match for it. They were simply crumbled down and after that just pushed away, the lifeless corpses of both Grant and Connie going with. Nothing solid could stand in its way, it seemed, so what could match the power of this beast?

The temple had been full of worshippers, but by this juncture it was emptying out, Cthulhu's followers retreating back into the arched spaces from which they had emerged. They'd helped to bring this monster here, had welcomed it with reverence and praise. But now they did not seem so sure and they were backing off from it. Would they be safe in those enclaves, though? It had already been established that mere solid rock could not stand in Cthalhia's way.

As for Gorsting, she was fully trapped. The creature she had summoned here had now become so bloated there was no way past it anymore. The poetess was still down on her knees, but with her back pressed firmly up against a wall. And the pleasure on her face was turning hurriedly to unnerved doubt and maybe even desperation too.

She had been the guiding force who'd engineered all this, however, and she tried to cling on to that fact. She lifted her chin proudly, knelt right up, then looked the being in its eyes.

"Cthalhia!" she called out loud, and she spread her arms again. "Perhaps you don't know who I am? I've been communing with Your noble spouse ever since I was a child, and am His greatest acolyte upon this world!"

The creature—which had swelled up almost to the full height of the temple now—paused a moment, going very still, its baleful marine gaze studying her.

"You would never even have arrived here were it not for me!" the poetess insisted forcefully.

A horrid, heavy gurgling sound came rumbling from Cthalhia's throat. She stretched two tentacles toward the woman's face until their tips were nearly brushing up against her high cheekbones. And Anastasia seemed delighted by that gesture, and she tipped her whole head forward so that she and the Old One were touching.

"There is *nothing* that I would not do for You, and *nothing* that I would not give. I even sacrificed my daughter so that You could come and liberate this world."

There was a soft purr to her voice, now, that was almost carnal in its depth.

"I love You and Your husband both. I love all the Old Ones, and would gladly …"

But she stopped. The tentacles had shifted and were on the move again. They wandered down to Gorsting's chin, then slid across it to her throat. And as I watched, they tightened round it firmly so the poetess's voice was choked right off. Alarm was rekindled on her face—she tried to pull herself out of that deadly grip, but she could not.

And pinned that way, she had no defense against what came next. One of Cthalhia's dense hind legs came rearing up above the woman. And it hovered for a moment, then smashed down. And the mighty force of that blow crushed the poetess to utter pulp, smearing her against the temple wall the same way that a small fly might be crushed against a windowsill.

It happened so abruptly that I reeled with shock. But that was just the start and there was worse to come.

ii

I thought at first it was my own nervous reaction to the horrors I had looked on in the past few minutes, my frame gripped by palsy and so trembling uncontrollably. But no, it genuinely was not that. The ground had started shaking underneath my feet.

Evidence of that was all around me before much longer. The outdoor lampposts shook as well, their glow reduced to a harsh quiver. The hedgerows round the garden were vibrating with a heavy thrum of leaves. The broken bits of glass beneath the windows were all jumping up and clattering around, and underlying all of that there was a slowly-rising shuddering sound.

None of the worshippers around me seemed to even notice that at first. They were transfixed by what had happened to their leader and they could not seem to take it in. They gawped, bug-eyed, and tilted their heads gently, gazing at her crushed remains as if they could not fathom what the Great Old One had done to her.

But finally the truth sank in, and panic swept through their dour ranks, bringing them back swiftly to their feet again. The ones round me were now stumbling back toward the house. And as for the ones below … trapdoors, hidden till this stage, came flying open in the lawn around the temple's rim and that whole crew came rushing out.

Tentacles were rising from the pit next moment, battening themselves to the ground above. A massive head began to lift up fully into view, its sickly green eyes hunting round. Cthalhia was coming out.

I was halfway mesmerized by that appalling sight, and should have become the next victim that she took. But, just as one of her long tendrils began snaking toward me, the ground abruptly lurched beneath my feet, and that made me stagger back and proper consciousness returned.

Sauquill Island seemed to be in the grip of a massive earthquake that was getting stronger all the time. Cracks were appearing in the brickwork back behind me and large chunks of masonry had started falling down. Except that retreating through the house was my one way out, and so I spun around and plunged back in and began racing through the lobby at full tilt, more fractures appearing in the ceiling and with dust and debris raining down on me.

By the time I'd reached the courtyard and was in the open air again, the violent tremoring of the terrain had become redoubled in its force and the house's roof had begun to collapse.

The horses were all gone by now, or else they were lying dead. Broken bits of carriage were strewn everywhere ahead of me. But the plain truth was that I was hardly on my own out here … the slaves of Cthulhu were still trying to escape, blindly scrabbling for the iron gate then pushing on quite mindlessly into the open ground beyond. I thought that I could make out

Cuesto in among them and also the Chinese maid, but their future was of no concern to me and I paid them little heed. Turning toward the shoreline, I saw that it was by this juncture far closer than it had ever been, the ocean's waters pushing across what had once been clear dry land.

The earth beneath me gave another jolt, so fierce this time it was practically as though the ground below my feet was trying to tip over on its side. The rumbling was lifting to a deafening roar, and so I kept on pushing forward till I'd reached the lane.

Whole trees were coming down out there, and the entire landscape was shaking with such force that nothing could stay still on it, the grasses swaying crazily and pebbles leaping up like small round bugs.

Then I heard a vicious crack and jerked my gaze in the direction it had come from. And I could scarcely believe what I was looking at. An entire section of this island's coast—including the beach which Brink and I had walked upon—had broken wholly off and sunk into the tide. There were only lashing waves where it had been, and they were attempting to reach further up.

And at long last I grasped the meaning of all this. Sauquill Island's time was done. It had served its purpose and was now returning to the green-tinged depths from which it had first come.

Which left what prospect for myself, since what dire fate awaited me? I could not swim the whole way to the mainland. It was much too far and I would never manage it. But then I recalled something else … the *Verona Fair* was still at anchor by the quay.

Praying to God it was still there, I began running toward Marinsberg. And I only slowed to glance back once.

Several massive tentacles were stretching across the ruins of the Gorsting house and ripping the iron fence away, and a vast shadowy body was proceeding after them.

iii

The whole time I was pumping my legs, I was terrified I'd not get there in time, because the ground was leaping wildly underneath my footsteps and that roaring sound was so loud its vibrations shook me to the core, the landscape lurching round me like some vessel in a storm.

But still I pressed on ... what choice did I have? Marinsberg appeared ahead, but not in any condition that I had seen it earlier on. Half of the place was already down, its eaves collapsed, its walls in ruins. And the rest was following suit, and seawater was rushing in along the cobbled avenues.

I kept on going, clambering over piles of brick and splashing through new rivers that were starting up. One house collapsed while I was passing by it, and it was only luck that saw its debris didn't bury me.

But finally, the quay came into sight. And Grant's white sloop—it was still there, tossing and chopping on the frenzied waves but its anchor still holding true. The fact that it had been moored a way off from the shore was no longer of any consequence, because the wooden jetty had collapsed, only a few upright struts still poking through the foaming brine. I glanced quickly around again and big cracks were appearing all along this section of the coast. And so I didn't even pause but stripped away my jacket, kicked my shoes off, dived into the waves and swam as strongly as I could.

The sloop was bucking so very hard I couldn't get a grip on it; every time I tried its hull rebuffed me and it almost struck me on the brow one time. But then I thought of yet another detail, and I breast-stroked around to the stern and found the rope to which the dinghy had been attached. And by that means I hauled myself onto the deck. When I looked back, the front section of Marinsberg and all the shattered houses there had started to subside into the depths.

I'd been on this boat a couple of years back and had even handled the controls. When I turned the largest key, the engine purred into life. The anchor was hoisted by a mechanized winch and so I threw the switch to start that up. Taking a hold of the wheel, I swung the craft around, and once its prow was pointed at the mainland I shoved the throttle forward and moved off.

The seascape out ahead of me was the most erratic I had ever looked upon and confusing to follow with the naked eye; the waves not only high and swift but traveling in different directions, each contrary to the others, so they crashed into each other with that savage force which can be only summoned up by Nature. The *Verona Fair* was lurching insanely and the wheel kept trying to tear itself out of my grip—I had to bring the whole weight of my body down simply to keep the sloop on course. And though I desperately wanted to, I knew in these conditions that I dare not push the boat too hard and kept it going at just two-thirds speed.

Which was a torture in itself. Every fiber in my being ached to get away from Sauquill and the awful horrors which had revealed themselves there. I kept my gaze fixed on the distant lights of the mainland ahead for what seemed an interminable age, thinking just of getting to that coastline and returning to a place where sanity still ruled.

I must have traveled half a mile by now. And, feeling slightly safer than I had, I glanced back in the direction I had come. And would have gasped if I had still retained sufficient breath. A scene of darkened hellishness was opening up in my wake.

The whole island was going under, its perfectly flat surface being swamped, its shattered rooftops disappearing and its fallen trees whirling round in eddies before being sucked down. It was hard to be quite certain from this distance, but I thought that I could make out living figures in among that chaos. A few of them appeared to be down on their knees again, with their arms raised the same way Gorsting's were. But most of them were milling around frantically. The waves closed over every last one.

And there was more activity along the sinking shore. Dark and heavy figures, in their hundreds too, were bobbing up from the tideline and pushing forward onto what had once been *terra firma*. Stouter-built than any human being, these were the same 'raiders' who'd attacked my house, a whole race of them by the semblance of it, emerging from the ocean's depths to reclaim what had once been theirs. Most of them were headed for the Plinth, the upper few yards of which were still above the waterline.

Then a different sort of motion caught my eye. My gaze went to the left, to the location Gorsting's place had been, and a tightness like a gasping talon fastened around my heart.

Moving at a crouch like some vast unwieldy arachnid, Cthalhia had grown far larger than the temple she'd been born in now, so enormous that she could have trampled Marinsberg to dust if it had still been there. Her ragged wings were standing out from her humped back. Her claws were grasping at the sinking ground like she was trying to tear it all apart. Inexorably and step by step, she was pushing herself toward the island's edge.

As I watched, she made the last few yards and then went sliding down into the lightless depths. And it wasn't very long before she was no longer visible, except there was a bow-wave where she had to be, and it was moving faster than before.

If she reached the mainland now? But in the situation I was in, that couldn't be my main concern. So that question was rapidly replaced by the single thought: *If she reaches me!*

Any caution was forgotten in a flash. I faced forward again and pushed the throttle the complete way up. The sloop started bucking so hard that its hull was almost lifting clear of the seawater below it. Spume from the waves up ahead was rushing over me in great cold swathes. But by this juncture I could almost *feel* Cthalhia behind me, so I pressed on for dear life.

Lurching in my field of view, the mainland was closer now and I could even make out some streetlamps that had to belong to the town of Narragansett. Less than a mile and I would make it to that place. I was still clinging to that whole idea, however, when a second bow-wave appeared up ahead. And it was swelling rapidly.

And was it being caused by Cthulhu himself? I tried to swing my rudder to the right and steer my way around the thing, except the wild opposing currents barely let me alter course.

This second wave got higher as it approached until a solid wall of water, near to fully ten yards high, was bearing down directly on me. When I shot a glance back to my rear, the exact same was happening behind. But then this thought occurred to me: *They are not really after me at all but simply moving close together, joining up. And I, irrelevant, am in their way.*

Which was something I tried to correct, straining at the wheel with every ounce of force. But all of this was happening too fast.

With a roar like a cannon blast, the two great waves loomed over me. They seemed to hang there motionless a second, but then they came crashing down together with incredible destructive power. I should have been engulfed and crushed, but thankfully the deck beneath my feet was shattered and the section I was standing on went splintering up. I found myself being flung into the air, performing a high arc before I splashed back to the surface. And I went a long way under, except then I struggled up until my gasping and half-blinded head was breaking through.

Fragments of the big white sloop were drifting all around me, but the two huge waves were flattening out. Only that something was replacing them. Where they'd met, a large whirlpool had now begun to form, and I could feel its suction start to pull on me, and so I swam away from it as best I could.

I mostly lost track of time's passage after that, just kept pushing on mechanically, barely sure if I was making any progress since the currents and the waves had me fully at their mercy. I went under again several times and I could barely see, there was so much salt caked in my eyes.

And sheer exhaustion finally began to take its toll. My arms were aching so badly that I could no longer extend them, and my lungs felt as if they had been filled with stones. A hot pain was working its way upward through my ribs. I trod water as best I could and tried to figure out where I was.

Were those some rocks that I could see? And closer than I had imagined, maybe only fifty yards away. Twin beams of light as from a pair of headlamps appeared briefly at the top, but then went out, plunging the whole scene into darkness yet again.

But this was my only hope. Ignoring the pain in my side, I tried my best to make it to the shore, grasping at the surface with numbed palms, trying to force some life into my weary legs, not really swimming at all but simply struggling against the tide.

I kept that up for perhaps a minute before accepting the plain fact I had not traveled any proper way. And I could barely keep the top half of my face out of the water now.

I wasn't going to make it, was I?

CHAPTER NINETEEN

THE WORLD
SHALL BURN

i

Incident Report by Erwin T. McMannis, a Sergeant of the Narragansett Police Reserve, Rhode Island, October 25th 1923:

At first, I waited for the man out there to make it the last distance to these rocks, but I quickly saw he was unable to achieve that goal. He was doing naught but floundering about, and increasingly feebly too. His head kept going down and taking ever longer to come back. I'd lived by the coast all my life and had seen near-drownings often, and I knew precisely what to do.

My hat and cape came off, and they were followed quickly by my uniform jacket and my gun-belt and my shoes. I did not dive in though—I had no idea of the depth of water out in front of me—but waded in until I was submerged to chest-height, then struck out. I might be a heavily-built man, some would say too heavy, but I am a practiced swimmer.

And I reached the helpless wretch in less than half a minute, turned him round so that his head was pressed against my shoulder, then kicked back to solid land. I hauled him out and, ignoring the harsh chill that was biting into me, laid him flat and then compressed his breastbone till he expelled water from his lungs. He began coughing violently.

His hair was hanging down across his eyes. I pushed some of it back and was immediately startled by the sense of recognition that gripped me. I knew this gentleman … I had met him before! This was—and I struggled for a moment to recall his name—Mr. Sinclair, the same fellow who had offered his help when we'd been searching for that missing couple.

Only that he was right now in a truly dreadful state, far thinner and gaunter than I'd seen him last, his cheeks sunk in, his eyes surrounded by dark rings, like he had spent the last few months in poverty and deprivation. Recovering from my shock, I tapped his face, trying to force him to come around, but he seemed barely capable of consciousness.

And so—left with nothing else to resort to—I picked him up between both arms and carried him back up the slope to where my wagon sat. We always keep some blankets in the back, and I bundled him up in a couple of those, wrapped one more round my own shoulders and then put him in the passenger seat while I went to recover my discarded gun and uniform.

Before much longer, we were setting off, and I was thinking of one matter above all the rest. We needed to dry off and put some fresh clothes on, or else—in this dire climate—we would succumb to pneumonia before too long.

Something very odd struck me, however, as I drove back up along Ocean Road. Where there were houses set along this street, several bursts of yellow flame had now appeared. And what could possibly be the cause of that? I had been on the constabulary for long enough to know that house fires in a town like this were rare, yet I appeared to be looking upon at least four of them simultaneously. And as I got closer to those flickering glows, I could make out there were people round them, out of doors in their front yards, and moving swiftly and frenetically.

They looked to be … actually dancing, or else capering about in the same manner as some pagan tribe. The drunken widower, Arthur Beeching, was one of them. And Mary Carver, the librarian, too. And there were several others that I recognized.

Some windows I passed by had been smashed up—I was not sure who had done that. And one whole part of Mary's roof was ablaze and the fire was spreading. All that I could do was gawp with disbelief, unable to grasp what was going on. And I would normally have slowed right down and stopped, but I was shivering quite hard by this stage and Mr. Sinclair looked half-gone.

I got us to the station house, dried myself off and donned my workday clothes. And then I rummaged in the lockers till I found some articles that he could wear.

He was finally beginning to return to proper sense. His eyes kept coming halfway open and I thought that I could see a pained and startled gleam in them. His face was slack and his jaw only moving limply, but he kept on mumbling the same one thing.

"Kuh-thoo-loo. Kuh-thoo-loo."

Which I was fairly sure was not a proper word at all. Perhaps he was delirious? I took hold of his chin and turned his face to me.

His blurry gaze came fully wide, and at first he looked petrified and started trying to pull anxiously away, like he was seeing something else and not a human shape at all. But then he focused and calmed down, although his lungs kept wheezing painfully.

"Where am I?" he managed to get out.

"Safe, and in the custody of the police."

"No! Nobody is safe, not with that thing around!"

I had no least idea of what he was referring to. A 'thing' … and could that mean a being not like us? I was starting to suspect this man was no way in his correct mind. But there were other matters at the forefront of my thoughts right now, the scenes of destruction I had observed coming here. What the cause of them might be I did not understand, except I knew it was my duty to go back and intervene.

"Mr. Sinclair," I tried to explain carefully. "Whatever it is you're trying to tell me, it will have to wait till later on."

And I gave him a brief outline of the chaos I had seen, the townsfolk acting crazily and wrecking their own homes. And expected his reaction to be *as confused as mine was now, but a look of comprehension gripped his features like he knew exactly what was happening.*

"Ecstasy and freedom!" he croaked in a harried tone. "It is the holocaust she said would come!"

And what sort of lunacy was this? The ordeal that he'd been through in the ocean's depths could not account for any talk like this, and so I realized it was possible that I was dealing with a madman here. I was trying to think how I could deal with that …

When loud and unexpected noises started drifting to my ears from the street outside this building.

ii

Strangled shouts that were barely human. Gibbering cries that were anything but sane. It was the parties at that dreadful house all over again, but amplified a dozen-fold this time. I could hear more windows being broken up, and mindless howls, and high-pitched simian shrieks.

This was some kind of frenzied riot I was listening to, a mob lost in mindless lawlessness and moving steadily this way. Feet were capering wildly on the paving stones, and by the sound of it—the crashes and the smashing sounds—they were destroying every object in their path, and they seemed to be fighting among themselves as well and hurling back and forth and rolling round.

The entire world shall be seen to burn.

And if Cthulhu's influence had genuinely been unleashed, then this could only be the start of it. This little township in Rhode Island State was merely the kindling for a conflagration that might well consume just everything, the Great Old Ones arisen again and plunging us into thoughtless, mindless anarchy. Except what else had Gorsting said?

"And once they have achieved that goal we shall be free of all laws."

Which had to mean that anything which represented law …

My heart froze up in my chest.

I stared at my new companion, and thought that I had never seen a man so absolutely lost in doubt and trepidation. His brow was deeply furrowed and his head kept jerking back and forth as though he could not tell if he was really dreaming or awake. This was a policeman in a sleepy coastal town, and without any warning the community he served had turned into a savage rabble and he could not start to understand it, let alone the reason why.

But I knew what the cause of all this was, and the urgency which came with that revived me fully to lucidity.

"We should either leave this place," I told the sergeant forcefully, "or else prepare to defend it."

"Why?" he almost shouted out.

"It is a place which represents the law, and so it will be destroyed. Forces far greater than you could possibly know are at work this night."

He stared at me blankly at first, like I was speaking in some foreign tongue. But then a piece of brick came smashing through a window right behind us, and that seemed to change his mind, and press him into action too.

Moving as dazedly as a sleepwalker might do, he went over to a cupboard at the back. It was padlocked but he found the key, opening the doors up to reveal three pump-action shotguns. And he took two out and handed one to me, then fetched a box of shells and we began to load the weapons.

The rioters had moved closer and were almost at the porch by now, shadows moving past the frost-rimed glass and a cacophony of shapeless voices pushing straight into this room. There was nothing we could do but stand and wait with our firearms at our hips, but McMannis kept on throwing anxious glances at me. These were his people, his neighbors after all, and he was obviously not sure if he could bring himself to shoot them down.

But once again, I saw the truth of this. A creature like Cthulhu would like nothing better than make murderers out of all of us.

The front doors of the station house shuddered briskly, and they started coming open.

But then they stopped and dropped back slowly. And the street beyond them went completely quiet.

CHAPTER TWENTY
THE MASTERY OF CTHULHU

i

Once that we had figured out the violence and the rage had stopped—and as quickly as it had begun—McMannis got me to the nearest hospital, where I spent most of the next week being treated for hypothermia and water in my lungs, but also for anxiety and shock. I have to admit I was not the easiest of patients. Waking from a nightmare, I would scream and thrash with utter, total lunacy, and even when I was awake memories came rushing back to me that drove me into states of frenzied agitation. The sight of Grant and Connie lying torn and dead and bloody on that temple floor. Katia being burnt alive. But most of all Cthalhia, her writhing face, her claws and bloated frame. Seeing all of that like it was happening again before my very eyes, I would moan and wail like some terrified child; they had to use morphine just to calm me down.

But gradually all that subsided, with my mind starting to heal itself. I was even able, near the end of that sojourn, to try and get a grasp on everything that had been happening outside this hospital since that unspeakable, unholy night.

The disappearance of a whole island was obviously the biggest news. Some of the papers even used the term 'Atlantis.' And the Navy sent some divers to investigate, but Sauquill was completely gone. The opinion of most experts, however, was this. New islands came up to the surface on occasion, seismic activity pushing them clear of the seas that had submerged them until now. So why should the reverse not also be the case, volcanism causing one of them to sink away again? The demise of its inhabitants was tragic—yes, of course—but just last month an earthquake had hit Tokyo and some three hundred-thousand souls had died. The planet that we walk upon can sometimes be quite merciless like that.

The loss of Grant and Connie made the headlines as well, naturally; it was assumed that they'd been drowned. But Anastasia Gorsting didn't get a mention, because no one was aware she had been living on that place.

As for the riots which had broken out—and they were not confined merely to Narragansett but had reached North Kingstown and Newport too and even started up on the fringes of Providence—officials who'd examined their details were divided as to their origin. Perhaps the massive subterranean turbulence which had made Sauquill Island sink had triggered something primal in the human brain, causing normally calm people to behave like animals for a short while?

But I could still remember stepping out onto that street with the shotgun in my rigid grasp and with McMannis by my side. There were hundreds of townsfolk out there, men and woman, young and old. They were no longer moving though, their heads still raised but their arms hanging limply by their sides. And each of their expressions ... it was precisely the same.

They were blinking like owls caught in harsh sunlight and were staring round at the destruction they had wrought, and every single one of them looked utterly amazed. Like someone else had done these deeds. Like they had left their bodies for a while, another consciousness replacing theirs. Eventually, they started clearing up the mess they'd made and putting out the fires.

And when I saw them doing that, I thought to myself: *It's all over. It is done with, and Cthulhu and his bride have failed.*

Except that I now understand I was completely wrong.

ii

Two weeks after I'd been rescued from the sea, I was settled in my fine apartment back in Boston once again. I was still having nightmares and was being plagued by awful recollections, but the knowledge we were no longer in danger helped to damp down all of that. I was trying my best to return to normality, my movements measured as I showered and shaved and then got dressed. And having accomplished that, I went through to the dining table, where my breakfast had been laid out for me.

Lying by my eggcup was today's edition of the *Boston Globe*, and I flicked through it idly as I munched my toast. And an item in the International Section somehow managed to catch my eye.

Apparently, there had been an attempted coup in—of all places—Munich, Germany. Some two thousand armed thugs had gone marching on the City Hall in an attempt to overthrow the local government. Gunfire had rung out and about a dozen lives were lost, but the police had driven the hooligans off and their ringleader was now in jail, arrested on the charge of treason.

Which I decided to take as proof that justice and the rule of law were still important in this world, despite what the poetess had attempted to do. This guy would in all likelihood be hanged, or else rot his life away inside some dreary prison cell.

Anastasia Gorsting had been wrong—her deities were nowhere near as powerful as she'd claimed them to be. They'd managed to affect some people's minds and cause a bit of carnage, yes, but it had been on a small scale and very short-lived too. How could nothing but a pair of ugly decapods enslave a world as big as this? They might still be there in the ocean's depths, but they were no genuine threat and were no longer relevant.

I set the *Globe* aside, finished up my coffee, then thought of going outside for a while, believing that a walk would do me good. It was one of those November days when the high bright sun gives us a brief respite from winter's clutches, the air crisp but the light warm so you were comfortable if you stayed clear of any shade. I started heading down toward the Common, and there was activity around me everywhere. Smartly-dressed people going in and out of coffee shops and stores. Shining new automobiles rolling by. Trolley-cars clanging and street vendors shouting out. What an age that we were living in, business booming, technology hard at work, and art and literature both coming to the fore!

And so, with a light heart and an easy stride, I crossed Beacon Street to reach the sward of grass beyond. And once upon it I strolled happily, my home city thrumming all around me and a cheerful smile lighting my face, because I knew that we were past the worst of it and all that lay ahead of us was progress and prosperity.

Only madmen wanted less, madmen like that German who had been locked up.

Whose name?

Was Adolf Hitler.

iii

It is thirty years later now, 1953. And I still have enormous wealth and still live in this grand apartment, except all my friends have drifted off and no one ever comes to visit me. And why precisely might that be? Because I'm utterly consumed with bitterness and helpless rage, and I even sneer whenever I recall my sense of optimism on that sunny day.

My first suspicions that I'd gotten this all back-to-front were aroused when that moustache-wearing lunatic was released after just one year. And we all know the course of events after that. His gradual then swifter rise to power, culminating in a deadly shadow that fell over almost all of Europe, and over much of the Far East as well. The persecution and brutality, followed by considerably worse, untamed slaughter and incessant madness consuming the world on which we strive to live.

The satanic rituals of the Waffen SS, devoting themselves to evil deeds. The death camps with their palls of smoke composed of burning human flesh. The hellish horrors—*worse* than Hell—of Stalingrad and Dresden and Nanjing. Towns and cities being pounded into rubble by strings of huge bombs falling from above, something that our kind had never seen. Almost eighty million people dead, more of them civilians than soldiers for the first time in our history.

And all of it for what precisely? Deranged fantasies of master races and the glory of the samurai. Not the product, not in any way, of rational healthy human minds but implanted in them quietly by a vast and monstrous intellect.

That night in Narragansett, when the rioting had broken out—it was Cthulhu fulfilling his original destiny, except his brand-new partner must have stayed his hand. *Why go this course, so brisk and crude, when there are subtler pleasures to enjoy, a longer game that can be played?*

In their sunken city, far beneath the rolling waves, Lord Cthulhu and his lady are not sleeping but awake. I know that because, even after all this time, there remains a telepathic link. I see them sometimes when I close my eyes and feel their presence constantly, still hidden from human gaze but plotting ceaselessly in the green deep.

And to them, this world has become nothing but a chessboard with two billion pieces and four billion squares, and those pieces are not called a pawn or rook. No, they have names like the Weimar Republic, the Reichstag, the Great Depression, Stalin, Molotov and Ribbentrop. And reaching out with their enormous mental energy, these two old gods take hold of all those pieces and they carefully and slowly move them round ... and the result is sheer calamity for us.

But nonetheless, it is my firmly-held conviction that that awful and demented war was not Cthulhu's final goal. His real triumph came neither at the start of it nor during its appalling course, but at its very end instead. Between one moment and the next, in that single instant when the mushroom cloud rose over Hiroshima—more chess pieces being moved around, called Einstein, Oppenheimer and Los Alamos this time—the world that we live in was altered, utterly and irrevocably.

We, our children and our children's children now live our entire existence on the very edge of a great bottomless abyss. One mistake, one slip, and we might tumble into it, and that abyss is called Extinction. Even as I write these words, the troops of China and the forces of the West are battling in the middle of Korea. And the Chinese do not have the Bomb as yet, except their friends the Russians do. One misjudgment is all that it would take. And it is in this way that every human on this planet wakes and sleeps and breathes and toils under the shadow of the Hand of Death. And what could please a pair of dark deities more?

In their sunken city in the ocean's depths, Lord Cthulhu and his bride lie with their tentacles entwined and their minds joined together, hatching plans so direly complex, so intricate and tortuously deceptive that no human consciousness could ever think them up. Time means nothing to these two Old Ones, and so they might continue with this game of theirs down endless horror-filled millennia.

Or else they might tire of it, decide to give the whole thing up, and end it in one blinding nuclear flash, the world burning just as Anastasia Gorsting promised that it would.

We think we have free will, but we are wrong.

No, we are all under the mastery of Cthulhu now.

ABOUT THE AUTHOR

TONY RICHARDS is the author of 17 novels and some 120 short stories. His fiction first began appearing in the Pan and Fontana Books of Horror, and he has since gone on to be a regular contributor to Weird Tales, Cemetery Dance, Black Static, Midnight Street, Asimov's SF and Alfred Hitchcock's Mystery Magazine, as well as numerous top anthologies. His work has been shortlisted for the Bram Stoker and British Fantasy awards and has been featured in several Best Horror collections. He has recently turned his attention to Lovecraftian fiction, with *The Howling Terror & Other Lovecraftian Horror Stories* being his most recent effort in that field.

You can find out more about his work at:
https://trfiction.blogspot.com.

ABOUT THE ARTIST

Steeped in the enthralling fantasy and science-fiction illustrations of the 1960s, '70s, and '80s, artist and illustrator **K.L. TURNER** brings a bit of old-school painterly style to today's methods. With more than 30 years of experience in the arts, he expertly brings an expressionistic style into his illustrations to create compelling works which captivate and draw the viewer in. His works are found in media and galleries around the world, and celebrated in pop culture.

A versatile creative type, Turner is also accomplished in the mediums of photography, sculpture, and the fine arts. Choosing to live and work on the beautiful front range of the Colorado Rocky Mountains where he was born and raised, he continues to derive inspiration from nature as well as cultural influences both at home and in his travels.

NEVER MISS A
BOOK YOU WANT!

Join the Weird House mailing list
for the latest news, releases, and special offers!

Scan this code or visit:
https://www.weirdhousepress.com/subscribe/

www.ingramcontent.com/pod-product-compliance
Lightning Source LLC
Chambersburg PA
CBHW030327020726
47493CB00004B/1183